the beggar's dance

the
beggar's
dance

a novel

farida somjee

Library and Archives Canada Cataloguing in Publication information is available upon request

ISBN-13: 978-1481892018
ISBN-10: 1481892010

Cover design by Zia Somjee
Cover image courtesy of Public Domain CCO
Author photo by Sadiq Somjee

www.faridasomjee.com

Printed and bound by CreateSpace in the United States of America

For Sadiq and Zia, my heroes

one

footpath
africa 1977–age 11

I DRIFT AWAY and start dreaming of such a life.

Mama yangu, my mother, frowns at me, squinting with intense effort. "Stop dreaming, you *maskini* boy." The anger in her voice reminds me that I am a *maskini*, a beggar, and I am not allowed to dream.

"Slouch and sit like a *maskini*, Juma," she whispers when an expensive car approaches the parking spot. Mama likes us begging on the footpath next to the ice cream parlour, a paradise for *Muzungu*, European, children, where their reality becomes my dream. Mama tells me, dreams waste our time and poison our souls. Dreams do not feed us. Seated against the wall of the ice cream parlour, I cup my palm and wait in anticipation. Coins drop, though not enough for a meal. Mama is still hopeful.

Children gather outside and lick different flavours of ice cream cones. They are lost in joyful conversation and laughter. Some of them sing to the music playing inside the parlour. I do not understand the words, but the voice is almost magical, the magic that I see through the eyes of these privileged children.

Once again, I drift away and start dreaming of such a life.

secret place
february 1977

DAYLIGHT TURNS INTO dark. The ice cream parlour closes by ten at night, then a quiet and scary time, not a single soul on the street, just Mama and me for now. We rush to the back alley to our secret hiding place and quickly climb to the top of the container that stores a backup generator for the freezers—parked next to the rear door of the ice cream parlour—where we sleep for the night. It is a blessing that the city is out of electricity every night. The darker the better, Mama tells me, less visibility for the thieves to spot us when they roam the alley. We cannot allow them to see us. In fact, Mama says, if possible I should not even breathe when they pass by. I wonder what a beggar could possess for them to steal. Mama says that they would use my body and hurt me. To distract myself from the constant fear, Mama tells me to gaze at the sky and allow the stars to magically hypnotize me to sleep. But I wake up to reality when a drunken man passes by. My breathing gets heavier. Mama quickly presses her hand over my mouth so I do not scream in fear. Eventually, the music of crickets puts me to sleep.

The morning stiffness for Mama is painful. It takes her a while to jump down off the container, and yet she never forgets to thank her God for another safe night. Her legs give in; she sits on the ground, rolls up her *kanga*, African shawl, and the torn slip underneath to massage her bare thighs, like kneading dough. Me, I stretch my arms and I am ready to start my day, but Mama can be sloppy and slow, especially in the mornings. I let her be and walk towards the adjacent street, one block west by the church, and sit by the doorstep. The heavy carved doors open and the black hinges squeak faintly. Sister Teresa walks out dressed in a nun's uniform, covered from head to toe with the exception of her tiny face. She smiles and signals me to come closer to her. She has shirts in her hand and stretches each of them over my chest for sizing. I remove my torn shirt and put on the new red one, which fits perfectly. She blesses me with certain prayers. I do not understand what it all means, but Mama always tells me that I must nod so the gods do not get angry with me.

Opposite the church is a school. The school ground is active and friends are happy to see each other. I give them an envious smile and lean against the wall by the entrance at the school gates. The school bell rings and the pupils rush to line up, looking disciplined in their starched uniforms—white shirts, white socks and white sneakers, girls in blue pleated skirts and boys in khaki shorts— while I remain alone waiting for Mama in my fancy new shirt. The school prefect closes the gate and the mean gatekeeper resumes his duty, holding a large branch to punish latecomers before he allows them through the school gates.

Mama finally arrives, dragging her feet. We walk to the end of the street by the berth. I run to the edge of the barge to have a closer look at the anchored ferry and admire her beauty. I dream of riding on it one day. The driver waves at me before carrying on with the daily maintenance so he can safely take the residents back to their homes in the evening. I envy the fishermen, street vendors and house workers who reside in their huts across the water. Someday, I will have my own hut and live there, too. Mama tells me that I should not think of the impossible. She says that the disappointment will only hurt me and I must accept who I am, a street boy, a beggar.

She hands me a toothbrush we found by the dump last week. We use the outdoor public tap by the entrance to the ferry berth to brush our teeth. We wash our faces, hands and legs. The water flow is weak; nevertheless, there is water, brown and not clear but still clean. Once refreshed, we head towards the town, passing by the little teashop that opens in the morning. Everyone greets the owner. "Kanji Bhai, *kemcho?* How are you?" Kanji Bhai hates us. "*Ondoka!* Get out!" He waves us away. We ignore the gesture and continue to stand our ground.

"*Naomba*, may I?" Mama says in a gentle tone, her palm outstretched for a handout. I hang my head in extreme sadness and hope for some food. To get rid of us, Kanji Bhai wraps some leftover food from the day before in a newspaper and asks his worker to give it to us, but many times he is in a bad mood and kicks us out empty-handed. We sit by the street corner and share three kebabs. I ask Mama to purchase bread but she does not have enough coins. Tears fill my eyes and the hunger is unbearable. "A little more begging, son, then I will buy it." She reminds me that not eating once in a while is okay; it trains our stomach to be stronger. She rubs away my tears with her *kanga* and feels the material of my new shirt. "Nice," she says and admires it. "Sister Teresa?" I nod, unable to speak because my tears have trickled down my throat, finding their passage to my heart. "Nothing for me?" I shake my head no. She feels my shirt again and smiles.

By late afternoon, the heat is too unbearable to walk around the town begging from shop to shop. We find a cool shady tree and go to sleep. Later in the evening, Mama counts the coins we have collected and gives me a smile. We stop at the bakery first and share half the loaf before heading to the street vendor to buy some corn. She hands me the entire corn.

"And you?" I ask.

"I am not too hungry today," she says.

I bite the piping hot corn, straight from the barbeque pit, and we walk back to the ice cream parlour.

Before the evening rush, the owner of the ice cream parlour, Mr. Smith, climbs up the ladder and changes the bulb of the outdoor fixture. He positions it towards our dark side of the path, and the parlour is brighter tonight. I thank him for being thoughtful. He gives me a serious nod without any eye contact and goes inside the parlour. I pick up the trash by the entrance and throw it in the dustbin to show him my appreciation. From the corner of my eye, I see a smile on his face, and this satisfies me.

"Mchh! Juma, stop it. You are ruining our chances," Mama says. "Don't help Mr. Smith." She carries on with her complaint, a mere excuse for me to sit next to her so she can collect more coins. When I do not listen, she raises her voice. "Everyone will think you work here and no one will give us money. Come next to me at once!" I give up and sit next to her. I frown exactly like her but fail to squint the way she does. She is not amused, and goes on and on lecturing me about the begging rules, which are *sit, slouch and look sad.*

This time, I stand up for myself and let her know that enough is enough. "Who makes all these rules anyway?" I ask defiantly.

She slaps me. "Are you arguing with me? Do you want Mr. Smith to kick us out of his footpath?" Her tone is harsh and the frown looks painful. She does not speak to me for the rest of the evening. In the meantime, I keep quiet and follow the rules like an obedient beggar.

A young *Muzungu* girl stands in front of me, staring as though she has never seen a beggar before. Her mouth is smothered with ice cream, and some of it drips down her hand and reaches her elbow. Her blue eyes sparkle when I smile at her. She almost drops the scoop, or at least I hope she will so I can catch it. "Why doesn't she give us money instead of standing in front of our faces?" Mama whispers. I am not pleased with Mama's behaviour. What if the girl hears her? I am relieved when the girl's mother comes by and takes her away, but the girl resists and refuses to step in the car. The mother squats at the girl's eye level and they talk for a while. They both go inside the parlour and get another cone. To my surprise, the cone is for me.

"*Ahsante sana*, thank you very much," I say and lick the ice cream before it melts away, ensuring not a single drip is wasted. The girl's mother drops a couple of coins on Mama's lap. Mama keeps her head low to show respect. When they leave, the girl looks through the car windshield and waves at me.

Towards the end of the evening, a regular *Wahindi*, Indian, family with six children comes by. They are loud and not as gracefully mannered as *Wazungu* families. Four of the children run into the parlour with their father. The mother, with her other two children, drops some change and a couple of homemade chapatti wrapped in a paper napkin on Mama's lap. "God bless you," Mama says. They get back in their car, parked in front of our spot, and stare at us. The mother hugs her children as though to assure them that they will always be well looked after. When they leave, Mama and I take a rolled chapatti each and enjoy our evening meal in our own private space. "Now, you would have not received this chapatti if you were roaming around. Follow the begging rules and you fill your stomach," Mama says, patting my back. However, she does not understand that my stomach is still empty. There is no more hope for today. The day has ended: it is dark and scary, not a single soul on the street, and once again we rush to the back alley to our secret hiding place for the night.

beach
february 1977

THE PIGEONS DISPERSE when the church bell strikes for the Sunday morning service. I look up to watch the bell swing from side to side. Mama places her hands over her sensitive ears until the bell stops. Then the service begins. Mama and I sit beneath the stairs at the entrance of the church and listen to the minister over the loud speaker that echoes through the open doors. The sermon in Kiswahili is bearable, but the *Muzungu* words that we do not understand seem to stretch for too long. Then something magical happens: the flock of pigeons return to the church windows when the choir and the music start. Mama and I thump our feet to the rhythm while we wait in anticipation of Sister Teresa sending out a serving of hot soup and bread, a Sunday ritual.

A man wearing a white outfit and white hat delivers

chicken soup filled with chunks of potatoes and peas, together with crusty bread on the side. "I will be back for the empty bowls once you are done," he says without any expression on his face and walks back into the church through the side kitchen door. I gulp down the soup and munch on my bread in haste before Mama finishes her share. I keep watching her. At first she ignores me and then gives me a *don't you dare* look, but I keep staring until she shares half of her piece of bread.

The church minister stands by the entrance, shaking everyone's hand and thanking them for attending the service. "Good day, Father. *Ahsante*, Father. Be well, Father Joseph. Heartwarming service, Father," are some of the Kiswahili responses I hear from the attendees. The *Muzungu* words exchanged have a rhythm of softness and gratefulness that makes understanding the language unimportant. On their way to their cars, the attendees gather for a short while and chat. A family of four gives us coins as they pass by. A group of young girls have the intention but run out of coins. "Oh, I used up my change for the church offering," they tell each other and walk away. We wait a while till everyone leaves before heading towards the bay at a relaxed pace.

We come across an *askari*, a guard, by the bank building. He jumps in front of us. Mama grabs my hand. She squeezes it tight, pulling me away at the same time, but the *askari* stops us with his stick. Even though I keep a brave face, I am terrified of him. He checks Mama all over with his cruel eyes and moves much closer to her. He presses her breasts. She slaps his hand and fights to walk away, but he blocks her and pinches one of the breasts sharply till Mama shrieks. I scream and hit him. He looks at me in disgust. Mama gathers her force and gives him a thrust on his chest, and we manage to escape. We run non-stop, not looking behind even once, but I still hear the sound of his malicious laugh ringing in my head. At last, we come to a stop and take a moment to catch our breath.

"You'll get us in trouble. What were you thinking trying to hit an *askari*?" Mama smacks my bottom.

"But . . ." I have difficulty speaking and I wrap my arm over my eyes.

"Now, stop crying like a *Muhindi* baby." She pulls my hand away from my face. I rub away my tears and walk with my head hung down. If only she knew that I had been trying to save her. I know what the *askari* wanted to do to her. I saw that before when I was much younger. We used to beg by the restaurant. At the end of the night, before closing, the waiters gave us leftover food. Mama fed me with her hand. Occasionally, I would pretend to bite her finger. It was like a game, and in return she would fake a scream and make me laugh. The street used to have an *askari* who was not nice to Mama. He threatened her with a wooden stick and asked her to come behind the restaurant after closing. Every night, Mama left me alone in the corner and went with the *askari* to the other side. I'd be so scared. She would squeeze me tight for the rest of the night, cry and rock me to sleep. One day she moved to the ice cream parlour and we never saw that *askari* again.

We reach the south side of the bay towards the entertainment area of town. Although the sun is directly on us, a cooling breeze brings relief from the heat. The cinemas are close by, and there is a new Hindi movie released every weekend. Street vendors set up snacks and refreshments by the parking area and wait for the *Wahindi* families to come by after the Sunday matinee show. I look forward to hearing everyone discuss the movie and sing the songs. Taxi drivers gather and play loud Hindi songs from the tape recorders in their cars as they wait for customers. I have learned to understand the Indian language and I enjoy the Hindi music. It is a perfect day to get free entertainment in this lively place. Sundays are by far my favourite days.

Mama finds a busy spot to beg. She allows me to be free and browse on my own. I hang around families with small children while they eat. One of the mothers gives me fried mogo from her share, while a man buys me a small packet of roasted peanuts rolled in a cone-shaped newspaper. Within a short time, I manage to collect some coins. *Mwizi* Samuel is always here. He approaches me and shows off how much money he has on him. "It's been a productive week, brother." Samuel fans the notes he carries.

My mouth falls open. "Lucky! You are so rich," I say.

He bonks my head with the base of his palm. "What do you have there?" I am embarrassed to show him the packet of peanuts and few cents I possess. He shakes his head. "Well, I will now celebrate my fortunes while you munch on peanuts. As for your coins, brother, I wonder what you could buy with them." He buys mishkaki and mogo. The aroma of mishkaki makes my mouth water. It is the most expensive skewered barbequed beef on the beach, and Samuel can afford it. After his meal, Samuel comes back to talk to me. "You see the riches you could make if you joined me as a partner. You can have a good life like me and eat mishkaki every day if you wish."

I look at Mama from the distance and her body language tells me, stay away.

I have known Samuel for three years, since I was eight. Mama says he must be about seven years older than me. We first met Samuel when he was wandering around the ice cream parlour one day. Mama was suspicious of him and he must have sensed it, so he came by and introduced himself to put her at ease.

She asked him the whereabouts of his parents. "I've never had a mother," he told Mama. "And *Baba yangu kakufa*, my father is dead." I remember the irritation in his tone.

"*Pole*, sorry. How did he die?" she asked.

"I mean he is dead for me. My father was a drunkard and used to beat me a lot. One evening he brought two women to our place. He smelled of Pombe beer as if he had taken a bath in it. The minute he saw me, he slapped me." Samuel's voice was deep and angry. "No reason whatsoever. *Bas, ka chapa*, that's it, just slaps." He clapped his hands, bang! I held on tight to Mama, ducking my head in her underarm. Mama was calm. She let him talk. Samuel settled on the ground next to us. "Then Baba, as usual, was rude and insulting. He told me to get out. That horrible beast!"

Mama was curious. "Where is he now?"

"I really don't give a shit."

"Watch your tongue," Mama scolded him.

"Sorry, Mama," Samuel addressed her respectfully. "But you would feel the same if you knew what he did to me that night."

"What happened?" Mama asked.

"I don't know what came about between the women and Baba, but one of the women ran out screaming and shouting without her top on, and her bare breasts were flying up and down, but she did not care." Samuel's eyes moved from side to side as he talked. "I hurried inside and saw Baba slap and kick the other woman."

I remember chuckling. For some reason, I found it funny. Mama asked me to keep quiet and let Samuel carry on the conversation. "Then?" she asked.

"I intervened and tried to stop Baba. In the meantime,

the woman escaped. Baba was drunk, angry and furious—
that bastard. He took a knife and slit my face. That was
the last time I ever saw him. He is a monster. I hope he
burns in hell."

Samuel walked for more than ten days until he reached
the city. Now he is far away from that monster, his Baba,
who can never find him. However, he cannot run away
from that five-inch scar on his face. Mama realized he was
trouble, so she politely asked him to hang around elsewhere. "Mr. Smith will not be pleased if we crowd his
footpath." That was her best excuse. Samuel did not
argue; he left and found his own spot and streets to hang
out. He refuses to beg. He tells me that beggars are losers.
They are people who have no ambition and give up on
life before they have even experienced it. So instead he
steals anything that is easy to grab and runs. He is a
mwizi, a thief.

"Nothing is spontaneous," he tells me. "Plan ahead,
have an escape plan, then steal and you never get caught."
He is definitely a good thief. "Be my partner, Juma. You
are a big boy now," he says, hoping I will agree this time.
I stay silent. "We could make a bigger plan together and
make lots of money." My silence frustrates him, but he
never gives up the question. I know I will hear it again
when I meet him the next time.

He secretly shows me gold jewellery he has stolen to
sell to the *Wahindi* women. They buy it off him; it is
cheaper than getting it from the goldsmith, but I am

pretty sure the women themselves have been robbed at least once and yet they support him. I am tempted with the idea of joining partnership with him. Getting training from a thief like him would be a great honour. Mama tells me that stealing is wrong and I should not listen to Samuel. But imagine being able to eat mishkaki every day. Just for that, it may be worth it.

monsoon
april 1977

GOD SURROUNDS US during the monsoon season. The
church provides us soup for the third day of Easter
holiday. The long rains arrive, creating the sound of
peace, and the air fills with the scent of sandy earth. The
fresh breeze in the city energizes the church attendees, and
many coins drop on our laps. I imagine heaven to be like
this.

The next day, after such a blessed weekend, Mama and
I settle by the busy shopping stores. People gather on the
pavement during the downpour, which lasts for several
minutes at a time. Laughter erupts on the street when one
of the cars stalls in a large flooded pothole. There is not
enough drainage, and the few drains that exist clog with
mud. There are no rules, and the drivers move in every
direction as long as they can safely pass through the road.

Mama's eyes sparkle as she joins the laughing crowd, and her teeth are so finely aligned that no one will believe she is a beggar.

"You look beautiful, Mama," I say, stroking her back.

She pushes me. "What beauty? *Maskinis* are the ugliest people. Don't flatter me with lies." She counts a shilling and slaps it on my palm. "Here. Take it. For the public shower."

I smile at her, understanding that she has accepted the compliment and here I am rewarded with a fresh shower.

Late in the afternoon, I notice Samuel running towards us as though someone is chasing him. I stand up to check if it is the police. He reaches us, out of breath, but no one is behind him. "What is the matter?" I ask.

"Juma, you will not believe this," he says.

"What?" I am eager to hear.

"Come check this out." He goes to the other side, under the tree. I follow him. He pulls a ring out his pocket.

"Is this a diamond?" I exclaim.

"Shh!" He puts his finger to his lips and whispers, "This is a jackpot."

"How did you grab it from the lady's finger?" I whisper back. I am worried. He is jumpy, too excited to talk. I say, "You relax, Samuel. You are worrying me, and you better not have cut the lady's finger."

"What? No, no, no, I didn't." He calms down. "You see, brother, this *Muzungu* lady at the café took the ring off her finger and put it on the table while she rubbed lotion on her hands. I walked past her table, grabbed it and left. She didn't even see me."

I shake my head in disbelief. "As easy as that?"

"See? A *Muhindi* would never do that. I suppose these *Wazungu* are not too smart, heh?" he says.

This time we both shake our heads in disbelief. I glance at the ring once more before Samuel puts it away. Then we both laugh until we are in stitches. Mama, as usual, gives me a nasty look and frowns.

"Do you enjoy starving?" Samuel moves closer to my face and speaks softly. "This ring will buy me ample food. Come on, brother. Now are you convinced that you should be my partner?"

"Why me?" I say, not sure if I should pursue the conversation.

"Because the work I need to get done requires a younger boy to be with me. It is big. It will make us a lot of money. So what do you say, brother?"

My heart speeds up like a racing car about to lose control. I get scared of what I might do. My mind says do, but my gut says don't. I close my eyes and sigh. I take a deep breath, in and out, as if I am trying to put the brakes on the racing car before it reaches the cliff. I sit quietly next to Mama, but I cannot help wondering what work could free me from the streets.

Samuel stands under the tree the entire afternoon, disappointed and refusing to talk anymore. "What's with him?" Mama asks. I shrug.

The silent treatment lasts for the rest of the day.

At night, Mama and I walk the streets catching flying termites swarming by the street lamps. We take them to the night vendor, who fries and salts them in exchange for a quarter of the catch. "Fair enough," Mama says, and the deal is made. We feast on the crispy termites before heading to the ice cream parlour through the dark streets.

On the way, we hear a screaming woman in the alley of the textile store. Mama starts to run away but I am already following the woman's frantic voice, not thinking of the consequences. "Juma, no!" Mama shouts, but it's too late. I am in the alley and Mama is coming after me.

A woman is lying against the alley wall, legs spread, her dress rolled up, screaming as though she has been thrown into a fire pit.

"*Aya.*" Mama rubs her head, and starts prancing.

The woman screams louder. Her eyes widen with every scream, sweat dripping down her forehead. Then she pauses for a while as though the demon has left her body and she is pain-free. But her breathing gets heavy and sweat fills her face. She starts to scream again.

I kneel down next to the woman; she grabs me hard. I am scared. "Mama, Mama," I shout.

"Get out of my sight." Mama pushes me out of the way and puts her hand in between the woman's thighs. She tells the woman to push harder.

The woman struggles, screams, sweats and yells at Mama—all at the same time. She seems confused.

"Well, push harder, you stupid woman," Mama yells back. "This is what happens when you spread your legs for fun. Now push. Come on. Push!"

Strange sounds come from the end of the alley. "Tell her to hurry, Mama," I say.

"Shut up. You should not have put us in this trouble in the first place," Mama says.

Suddenly, the woman lets out a long scream—she does not stop until part of her baby's body slips out.

I feel sick.

Mama fiddles around trying to pull the baby out completely, but he comes out dead. She drops the baby on the woman's chest and abruptly stands up.

The woman cries in agony, with her baby tightly pressed against her breasts. Blood is everywhere.

Mama grabs my hand and we run out of the alley.

"No one"—she slaps me hard—"no one will follow our screams and neither should you. Never do that again."

I vomit on the street. Without sympathy, Mama grabs my hand again, pulling me roughly, and we head to our secret hiding place.

With the rain pounding on the plastic cover over me, I think of Samuel, the partnership and the comfort of living in a safe hut. It all makes sense. All night in my sleep, I hear the woman's scream, and I see the dead baby and the blood. I do not want to witness anything like this again. I must speak to Samuel.

~

Mama notices my silence the entire morning and tries to comfort me. "I don't want to talk about last night. Just leave me alone," I say.

The vendors grab their things and take cover next to us by the building when they hear the thunder. I look up at the rain clouds to check if I can see God. Mama tells me that God hides way above the clouds playing football; every roll of thunder is a sign of God scoring a goal.

The long rains continue to pour. I step on the pavement and allow myself to get drenched. "If you are hearing me, God," I pray, "please wash out my last night's memory with your divine rain."

Just then Samuel passes by. And the rain stops.

"Samuel," I call out at him.

"I am done with you, Juma," he says. "It's time we were not friends anymore. Now go on." He pushes me away. I can tell from his voice that he means it this time, and I fear that I will never see him again.

"I will do it, that's what I want to tell you," I say before he gets any more upset.

"You will do it?" He lifts me up. "Good decision, brother." He drops me back to the ground.

Mama approaches. "Do it what?" she asks. I say nothing and hang my head down. She grabs my ear, pulls me away from Samuel and scolds me. I do not say anything, I keep quiet. Samuel comes closer to us and tells Mama that she should let me go and he will take good care of me. Mama is angry with Samuel. "Get away from him. I don't want to see you talk to my son again." She slaps him.

"You have to make the decision now, brother," he tells me with a palm pressed to his cheek. "Come with me and leave Mama forever or I will never see you again."

This is not fair at all. The slap may cost me my freedom, but I cannot leave Mama; she will be scared without me. Maybe someday I can convince her that it is okay to work with Samuel. He is my only chance, my only hope. I know I have committed to my friend and I will keep my word. But today is not the day.

mama
october 1977

I WRAP MAMA'S *kanga* over her shoulder to comfort her from the shivers. Every so often, I hear her teeth chatter, or a grunt whenever she jolts. I hold on tight to her so she does not move towards the edge. In the middle of the night, her body breaks into sweat. I feel the heat from her burning body as it touches mine, as though I am standing next to the charcoal pit at the barbeque vendors' spot. Ignoring the discomfort, I hang on tight. What else can I do? It is too dangerous to find help at this hour. This has been the longest night of my life.

As soon as it is dawn, I ask Mama to climb down. It takes her a long time to hang her body over the container. She loses her grip and drops hard to the ground. I stretch her body and massage her legs and hands to relieve the pain. After a while, with much effort she manages to crawl to the front of the parlour.

I run to the bay and wait for the morning ferry to arrive. I am hoping that Samuel will be able to help us. He has refused to talk to me for the last two seasons. Every time we have come across each other, he has looked the other way. So many times when I tried to say hello, he snubbed me and walked away. I know he is still my friend and he will help me when he finds out how seriously sick Mama is.

Samuel finally arrives. I rush to him and grab his arm. "Hey! How dare you," he says and pushes me away.

"Mama is very sick, Samuel. Help us, please," I say.

He makes an aggressive stop. "You betray our friendship and now you decide to come to me for help?" He kicks at the stone by his foot so he won't have to look at me.

"Please, my friend, help us. I don't know anyone else." My voice trembles. I run towards the parlour and do not give him a chance to say no. He follows me.

"Mama," I call her in a soft voice. "Samuel is with us, he will help." Her body is limp and she is unable to talk. I touch her forehead with my palm; the fever is still high. "What shall we do?" I ask Samuel.

"You have to take her to the government hospital. It is the only free hospital, but that is too far, brother," Samuel says. "The taxi will be costly. You may not be able to afford it." I untie a knot from the edge of Mama's *kanga* where she saves her begged money and hand it over to Samuel. "What is this? This will not even get you beyond two streets." He drops the coins on the ground in disgust.

"Help me, please!" I plead.

"I do not have space in my heart to pity people like you. You should have joined my partnership and you could have saved your mother."

I kneel and touch his ankles, begging him to help us. "I will pay you back." Samuel pulls his foot away from my hands and walks away without a word. "Samuel! Samuel!" I call out after him as he disappears in the distance.

"I will be fine, my son," Mama manages to say with barely any strength in her voice. "Let me stay here for the day." She crunches her body further and goes to sleep.

"You need to see a doctor. I will find you help, Mama," I assure her.

I knock on the front door of the church. I know it is closed at this time of the day, but I take my chance. To be sure, I check the side door, knock and call out to anyone. "Help! Help!" There is not a soul in the building. I am sure God is. After all, it is God's house. But God does not help me.

In a short while, the school gate opens. The parents dropping their children do not stop for me, and everyone is in a hurry. The mean gatekeeper notices my panic. "What is the matter?" he asks politely. Surprised at the softness in his tone, I tell him about Mama, even though I am quite scared of him. "Just wait here. I will tell the headmaster to phone for an ambulance," and he goes to the office area.

I glance at the church and apologize to God. "I am sorry I doubted you. Thank you."

In the meantime, latecomers take advantage of the gatekeeper being out of sight. One of the pupils sticks his hand through the gate bars and slides open the lock. They all give me a thumbs-up and rush directly to the assembly line. I wait by the gates in anticipation. After the school assembly, the gatekeeper comes back with one of the *mwalimu*, teacher, who offers to help. "Forget the ambulance, son. It will never arrive. I will take you in my car." The gatekeeper slides both the gates open for the *mwalimu* to drive out of the parking area. "Ask the head monitor in Standard 5A classroom to keep the pupils quiet," he says to the gatekeeper. I run to the front of the parlour and the *mwalimu* follows me in his car. We pick Mama up from the footpath. Twenty minutes later we reach the hospital. The *mwalimu* helps me take Mama out of his car and drops us by the entrance. "Good luck, son. I am sure she will be fine," he says.

"*Ahsante, bwana*, thank you, sir," I say.

Mama sits at the doorstep. "I will wait here. You can get the doctor," she says.

I enter the hospital; it smells like a mixture of medicine and Dettol. There are many people queued up at the admission window. I worry about Mama being all alone by the doorstep, but I am afraid to check up on her or else

I will lose my turn in the queue.

At last, almost two hours later, longer than I expected, it is my turn. "*Sema*, go ahead," the admission clerk says.

"My mama is sick. She needs to see a doctor," I say.

The clerk is not friendly at all. "Fill up this form and describe what is wrong with the patient."

"She has a fever and needs to see the doctor. I do not know how to read or write," I say.

"Well, figure it out." She is rude and throws the form at me. "Next!" And I am shoved to the side.

With the form in my hand, I rush out to see if Mama is okay. She is fast asleep. I stroke her forehead and tell her to wait a little longer. I ask the nurses passing by to help me fill up the form, but they seem busy and in a rush, and probably they do not even see or hear me.

"Excuse me, sister," I say to yet another nurse. This time, one kind nurse pays attention to my request. She follows me outside to check up on Mama. "Good lord, she has a high fever," she says and sticks a thermometer in her mouth. She checks her pulse and jots down the results—I assume—at the back of the form on a blank sheet. "What is her name?" she asks.

"Mama," I say.

She stares blankly at me for a while, and I hope she hurries up. "Okay, I will write a fake name and a fake post box," she says, "so you can have a turn to see the doctor. Also, show the doctor my notes at the back of the form." She asks me a few more questions about Mama's symptoms, then brings a hospital wheelchair and helps me take Mama to the waiting area, where we settle her on the bench. The nurse hands the form to the doctor's receptionist. I sit on the floor next to the bench and wait for Mama's fake name to be called out. "Find out her name when she feels better, okay?" The nurse teases me and laughs as she leaves, pushing the empty wheelchair. I do not know why finding Mama's name is so important, but I agree.

At about four thirty in the afternoon, the doctor attends Mama. She is admitted to a room for the night where more doctors and nurses fuss over her. "Hold my hand and do not worry. Everything will be fine," Mama tells me. They give her an injection. I squeeze her hand tight and do not let it go. Eventually, Mama falls asleep. She looks like an angel in the bed. All the other five patients in their beds, in the room, are sedated as well and are not conscious of their surroundings. The doctor advises me to go home and come back the next day. I ask him if I can stay with Mama, but he refuses. I hide behind the bathroom door. At night when all the lights turn off, I sneak under Mama's bed and sleep there. The ceiling fan keeps the room cool, and I lie on the cold cement floor with ample space to stretch. It feels comfortable.

In the middle of the night, I hear a loud beep from the machine that has been hooked up to monitor Mama. The nurse hurries into the room to check on her. I startle her when I come out from under the bed. First, she screams and then she ignores me; she does not have time to deal with me. She rushes to get the night doctor on duty. He takes two flat blocks, puts them over Mama's chest and snaps them. He repeats this a few times till the machine lets out a long continuous beep. The nurse looks at me and blinks her eyes. I question her with a frown; I do not understand. She ducks her head down. The doctor closes Mama's eyes and covers her face.

Mama yangu is dead.

I do not know why! The doctor does not feel it is worth his time to explain. He signs the chart and leaves.

"No! No! Mama! Mama!" I scream and jump on her bed. The nurse pulls me away and takes me into the waiting room. She comforts me. In the meantime, two men come along and take Mama's body away. The nurse asks me if I have any place to bury her, or they can arrange a traditional burial on the land provided by the hospital for a minimal charge. I explain to her that I have no money. She suggests they take care of it at the morgue. They have a room to cremate bodies that are left unidentified. I have to let them do that. Where else can I take her?

The nurse walks me to the morgue section and goes back to her ward. I twist the knob and bang on the door. Mama is already locked in, and she must be so frightened to be alone. I sit and lean against the door for the rest of the night and wait for it to open so I can go check on her.

Instead, in the morning, one of the men hands me Mama's ashes wrapped in her *kanga*. I cling to her ashes and walk out of the hospital. I roam the city aimlessly all day. My mind feels empty and my heart is paining. I do not know what to do with myself.

Eventually, I reach the bay. Samuel comes running to see me. We stand still in front of each other. I have no words to say. He knows. My eyes burn and I look away. He moves forward and touches my shoulder. "*Pole rafiki,* sorry, my friend," he says. I push him away and walk down towards the shore. I untie Mama's *kanga* and let her ashes free into the ocean. The sun shines over the ashes like the speckles of glitter. I give a last glance at Mama's beauty. "Be well, my angel, be well."

Samuel stands next to me. "Come along with me, Juma. You deserve a good life," he tries to convince me.

"Go home, Samuel. You'll miss your ferry." I do not want to talk to him, look at him or confront him. He is not worth it. I leave him standing alone.

Instead of going back to the ice cream parlour, I go to the spot where Mama used to sit me on her lap when I was little. She would snuggle me close to her while waiting for passersby to drop coins into a small tin bowl she kept next to her. I think that was the last time I remember her hugging me. How I long for that hug one more time. I sit on the footpath and kiss Mama's *kanga* with her scent still present. Tears roll down my cheeks. No one cares. I am on my own.

street
march 1978

IN THE LAST few months, I have discovered ways of surviving alone on this new street. I spend most of my day outside the shops of the main building, my new footpath where I feel welcome. The roofless car garage in the alley behind the main building is my night sanctuary, my new secret place. No matter how lonely and frightening, it has kept me safe. In the morning, I wake up and salute the sun. I am grateful for the sun; it gives me hope that after every scary night it will rise to brighten me. I hide behind the tree inside the garage next to the entrance when Sanju Bhai, the owner, pushes the screeching gates open, leaving a circular mark on the ground from the rough wheels. He bends his lanky body like a rubber band, touching the earth, and kisses his hand before entering. The cars in the garage await his magic touch. I hear people say that he has a hand of steel; no one can fix cars like he does. His mouth moves from chewing tobacco, and a fresh pattern of spit splatters the side wall. He reaches inside the gunny sack hanging over his shoulder for incense and a match-box. The strong scent lingers as he walks around with the burning incense and recites "Om Shanti Om" to bless his day. I take this opportunity to tiptoe from behind the tree, out to the streets.

I tuck Mama's rolled-up *kanga* under my arm and ask her to walk the day with me. Her presence is in my heart, in my spirit, in my memories. She is my *angel*. She speaks to me in every breath I take. "Be brave, my son," she says. I press her *kanga* against me and smile. She is happy that I have moved to this busy main street at the heart of the city, away from the quiet street by the ice cream parlour where the nights are much longer, quieter and scarier. She is happy that I have walked away from Samuel and do not hang around the entertainment sections as he does. The morning noise of the cars, the congestion at the roundabout, and a driver swearing and honking at a pedestrian running for his life are just the beginning of this busy street. Workers head to their sophisticated offices and banks. One of them, a man dressed in a white shirt and blue tie, greets me but does not wait for my response. A group of women in fashionable dresses, with strong perfumes, are lost in conversation.

I stand in front of a restaurant owned by a strict lady, Jena Bai. She arrives in a taxi. One of her workers takes the basket she is carrying, while another takes her keys to open the restaurant. Sanju Bhai comes running out of the garage and gives Jena Bai the good news that the spare part he has been waiting for has arrived and he will be able to fix her car today. She grumbles about the cost of the taxi and other things, until Sanju Bhai makes an excuse about needing to place an urgent phone call and leaves. "*Ya khuda!* Oh god!" She steps into the restaurant with a big sigh, as if she is complaining to God. I am not sure why she is always unhappy. And her Kiswahili is terrible. She claims to have been born here, yet she cannot speak the language.

The butcher next to her restaurant, a kind and pleasant Swahili man who serves only halal meat, starts his day by saying *bismillah*, in the name of Allah, at his doorstep. He wears a colourful checkered *shuka* wrapped around his waist. I think he carries a lot of luck, so I make sure to pass by him at least once a day, whenever I get a chance. A full load of freshly skinned cows arrives in a pickup. One by one, the cows are hung on the thick hooks clamped to the rod inside the butchery. The scent of women's perfume mingles with the smell of raw meat. Within thirty minutes, the sound of the meat-cutting saws echoes in the street.

Sushmita's father drops her at work by ten. I offer to hold her bag and tiffin while she opens the dispensary next to the butchery. Patients have already arrived to get their number to see the doctor. I place her things on the table, and she turns on the lights and air conditioner. She opens the tiffin and gives me *aloo paratha* for breakfast. I like her. She once gave me some quinine for my shivers. "Don't mention it to anyone," she said. With my finger on my lips, I nodded. To return the favour, I offered to do her chores, such as picking up some vegetables from the *sokoni*, market. Instead, she asked me to pray that a suitable boy chosen for her agrees to marriage. By half past ten the doctor arrives. He parks at the same spot every day and, before going into the dispensary, leans against the door of his car for a moment deep in thought. Then he nods at me and walks into the dispensary carrying his black briefcase.

I settle on the footpath next to Mama Fatima's hair salon, which happens to be my favourite spot. Begging is easier because women are more compassionate, and after their grooming, they seem to be more generous. Maria, a middle-aged African woman who works for Mama Fatima, cleans the salon. Her first customer arrives for hair braiding. She concentrates on each strand and ties colourful beads to it, turning the customer into a dazzling beauty. Mama Fatima arrives late. "Maria, I have a headache today. Prepare a hot cup of chai," she says, pressing her forehead. By noon, the salon is busy and I have collected enough coins to purchase a couple of bananas from the vendor selling fruits to the shopkeepers. I move closer to the restaurant during lunchtime. A kind lady hands me leftover chips wrapped in a newspaper, and

I am all set for my afternoon meal. Jena Bai leaves at two and drives home in her car, which Sanju Bhai has finished repairing. She will return later for the evening shift when the restaurant is the busiest. The rest of the shopkeepers close at five.

Above the shops is a motel. The motel bar at the corner opens for the night, blasting music so loud you can hear it to the end of the street. The night ladies gather in their colourful dresses, with lots of makeup and perfectly braided hair—mostly by Maria—and stand near the pole for their male friends to come by. Many times they make their man give me a few coins; this has become part of the ritual of negotiating their price. They talk to me and give me safety tips. "Stay away from the gullies. Evil men hide in there. They will grab you and hurt you." No matter how much I try to control myself, the drips of *susu*, pee, wet my shorts out of fear. I walk away in shame and sit in the corner by myself. The night ladies chatter, looking directly at me, then go on with their business. The next day, one of them brings me an old shirt and shorts and sneaks me into the bar's toilet to change. When I come out of the toilet, she gets emotional and cries. "You look good, you look good," she says and walks away without giving me a chance to properly thank her. I look for her by the poles, but she is nowhere to be seen. Later on, I find out that her estranged husband stole her son last year, pretending to take him to the cinema but never returning. "Finally she parts with her son's clothes," one of the night ladies tells me. "Let's hope she finds peace now."

By the end of the night, the night ladies and their male friends are drunk, and they go upstairs to the motel room to do their monkey business. A versatile street this is. There is a total transformation from day to night. At midnight, the restaurant and bar close, the street lights dim and everyone leaves. I quietly walk upstairs to the end of the motel balcony and slide down the gutter pipe to the garage. I truly lucked out with this secret passage. My angel led the way the night I tried to climb over the garage gates and cut myself on the sharp broken glass glued to the top of the gates. The gates are secured with chains and padlocks, making it impossible to steal the cars. There is a trace of Sanju Bhai's distinctive body odour, as pungent as a jackfruit, throughout the garage. I bunk myself in the back seat of one of the cars and cling to Mama's *kanga*. The frightening moment begins and a spooky silence sends shivers up my body. In the middle of the night, I hear the squeak of a mouse followed by a big clang, and then it is quiet again. A sharp pain shoots up my nerves. "I miss you, Mama," I say, and kiss her *kanga*.

"I am with you," my angel says.

I hang on tighter to her *kanga* and chant as though in prayer. "Put me to sleep my angel, put me to sleep my angel, put me to sleep my angel."

The next day, Sunday morning, I wake up before dawn and climb up the gutter pipe, as the garage remains closed. The pipe moves with my weight and I worry that one of these days it may crack and I will get into trouble. My angel tells me not to worry, I will be just fine. The early morning silence on the street makes me feel lonelier than I already am. The regular stray cat is the only company I have. I hide under the motel balcony stairs for an hour before the sun rises. I thank the street for looking after me and keeping me safe for another night.

This vibrant street has a lot of energy, a lot of hard work, a lot of kindness, a lot of sadness, a lot of laughter and a lot of pain. No matter what it has, it is my home, my new home, and I like it.

a great spirit
may 1978

A *MUHINDI* BRIDE transforms into a beautiful princess when Mama Fatima styles her long silky hair into a bun, pinned with studs of rhinestones. I sit outside the doorstep and listen to the bride's conversation. A couple of her friends tease her about the groom. "He is going to be busy removing these studs tonight," one of the friends says. The bride covers her face and looks away.

"Look at her blush," Mama Fatima says. "And what a beautiful dark *mehndi*, henna, on your hands. You know what that means, don't you?" The bride shakes her head no. "It means he loves you very much."

Her girlfriend pushes a needle through a lemon and gives it to the bride. "I know you couldn't care less about this ritual, but please keep holding the lemon. You cannot afford evil eyes today."

When the cheerful bride leaves the salon, she sneaks a five-shilling note into my palm and closes my hand into a fist as though she does not want her friends to see. "Go celebrate," she says and winks.

I rush to the restaurant. My rubber slippers squeak on the greasy floor, making an annoying sound as I walk to the counter. Not that anyone notices; after all, the place is noisy enough. The waiters rush from table to table. They are rough with the plates and jugs of water, but the happy customers do not seem to be bothered when the water spills on the table. I order a plate of *pilau* from Jena Bai. "No, it is six shillings," she says in a firm tone.

"Please, Mama, I have only five. Scoop two spoons out, please," I say politely.

"*Mimi na fanya bizinesi we shenzi maskini.* I run a business, you stupid beggar."

The woman queued behind me takes a shilling and slams it on the counter. "Now, give him the food," she says.

Jena Bai gladly takes the shilling and serves me lunch. "Don't come again if you don't have enough." She points at the door. "Now, go eat outside, not inside the restaurant." People around the counter laugh, including the woman who slammed the shilling. I sit by the corner of the garage to enjoy the *pilau* and send my prayers to the bride: *May you be blessed with a happy life.* I chuckle to myself and wonder how long the groom will take to remove those studs tonight.

~

"*Jambo*, hello," Mama Fatima's daughter says. She comes to the salon every Saturday and never fails to greet me. She is a great spirit—I sense it—and a cheerful person. Afterward, her friend visits, and they lean against a street parking sign across from the salon. Chuckles and giggles. They cling to one another, exchange conversation, reach their palm over each other's ear and whisper. More giggles. I feel envious of their friendship, of how happy they seem, a friendship no beggar could imagine having. Mama Fatima's daughter runs back into the salon and convinces her mother to allow her to watch an afternoon Ladies Show. The two friends hold hands, run across the street towards the petrol station and eventually disappear from my view, on their way to the cinema hall.

The following week, Mama Fatima's daughter comes by for a haircut. Her long, black, straight hair is now as short as a *Muhindi* boy's hair. I do not like it. I do not know why she would do that. I stand up with my mouth open and stare at her when she walks out of the salon.

She stares back. "Do you not approve?"

"Sorry, *Dada*, sister. I did not mean to stare," I say.

"Zakiya, my name is Zakiya," she says and sits down on the path criss-crossed. I am stunned by her behaviour. "Go on, sit down," she demands. I cautiously sit next to her. Mama Fatima would kill me if she saw this. I glance inside the salon to make sure Mama Fatima is not watching. Dada Zakiya asks me why I waste my time on the streets and do not attend school. I tell her that I am a *maskini*. She keeps quiet for a moment, as though deep in thought, and then sighs. "Why are you a *maskini*?"

"I was raised a *maskini*," I say. What a stupid question.

"So now you've become one by choice. How ridiculous is that?" She is rude and tough on me, but I am not going to let her win this argument.

"My mother was a *maskini*, so I am a *maskini*. It is not a choice." I hope she will leave me alone.

"Hey, guess what? My mother is a hairdresser, right? Right or wrong? Come on, answer me." I am shocked and do not answer. "But I'm going to be a doctor and a bloody good one. Yes, it is a choice, you idiot." She shakes her head, gets up and takes off.

I am speechless.

Dada Zakiya comes back after an hour with a book and drops it on my lap. I take the book and look at her. "This is for you," she says, smiling. "It's a picture book with a few words. Read and make up a story. I will be back next Saturday and you can tell me the story."

"I do not know how to read." I reach up to return the book.

"I said make up a story. Listen and learn," she says and pushes my hand away.

"*Ahsante*, Dada Zakiya." I thank her and hold the book close to my heart.

"*Kwaheri*." She waves goodbye.

I am glad she leaves on happier terms this time.

I begin to love and hate Dada Zakiya. Regardless, I give the book a chance. The pictures are funny. I make up the story as I see it. The dog is the master and a little boy is his student. The dog seems to know what is right and wrong; he shows the little boy the ways of life. It is strange. How can a dog behave like that? I am confused—what a strange book—but then that is what the story seems to be. I read the book over and over again for the entire week, and each time the story gets more intriguing.

A week later, Dada Zakiya comes by in the afternoon, with her usual tomboyish look, wearing jersey and jeans. I wonder if she wished to be a boy. With her short haircut and dressing style, she is not as graceful as the other *Wahindi* girls, but she is very pretty.

"*Jambo,*" she says. "Do you want to tell me the story?"

"Yes, Dada, I want to."

"All right then, follow me to the back of the shop so no one sees us." We sit behind Mama Fatima's parked car. Dada Zakiya holds her chin in her palm and listens to my story as I narrate it to her. "That is a lovely story. I wish I had a dog," she says.

"No, Dada, this is not real. Real dogs are very vicious. They can bite and kill."

She laughs at me as though I do not know much about dogs. Then she points her finger at the letters in the book and makes me repeat the sounds after her. "Are you enjoying learning?" she asks.

"I am having so much fun." I give a flying kiss to the book.

"This is what school is like. Our schools are free, and you should be attending them instead of begging," she says. "But I know that we have to pay *magendo*, bribe, to the headmaster for the enrolment, so it can be difficult."

"Yes, Dada, and also I need to beg during the daytime or else I will not have money to buy food."

"Where do you sleep?" she asks.

I tell Dada about the car garage and how I sneak in there at night. She seems impressed with me. She asks me so many questions that I think I must end up telling her my entire life story, and before we know it, it is late in the evening. We hear Mama Fatima close the salon and walk out the back door. Both Dada Zakiya and I sprint out of there and stop at the end of the alley to catch our breath. We have a good laugh at the same time.

She tells me that she will bring me more books and teach me how to read and write for at least an hour every week. She also promises to bring me a clean t-shirt and some homemade food. I nod as she speaks. "But you must take a wash and clean that mucky face of yours," she says, wrinkling her nose. "You have gunk hanging down your nose too."

I am embarrassed, but at least she is honest and she is right. I know I have to go to the public bathroom and scrub myself with scented *hamam* soap, which will cost extra. I will try to eat less this week and save the money.

"I will, Dada Zakiya. I will be clean for you the next time you see me," I assure her.

"Good. Uh, what's your name?"

"Juma."

"All right then, Juma. This will be our secret," she says and runs across the street to get home before Mama Fatima does.

Dada Zakiya tells me that I am a fast learner. In just over six months, I can read plenty of words. She finds me entertaining and laughs when I try to read some words that are difficult to put together. At the same time, she tells me not to worry about my accent. I do not have to sound like *Wazungu* as long as I can speak and read English. This way, I will be able to find a good job. It turns out that she has a plan for me. First, I have to become taller and bigger, so I need to wait to grow up anyway. In the meantime, I must study hard and become smarter. Later on, she will ask her friends' parents to find me some work as a waiter in a classy beach hotel.

"You will receive tips from the tourists and get to wear a nice clean uniform," she tells me with such enthusiasm. I dream and gaze at the clouds. "My mother should not find out about our plan at all," she says.

"I will not tell anyone, but I do not want you to get into trouble because of me."

"No trouble, my friend. In about two years, you will

be ready for work and I will be way gone from this country to become a doctor, so don't you worry about me."

I blink my eyes. What does she mean, not be in this country for too long? I feel like someone is ripping my heart out of my body. I want to stop it but it keeps ripping. Why me, God, why me? I feel as if I am losing my mama all over again.

library
may 1979

"NOW REMEMBER TO behave like an obedient student," Dada Zakiya says. She hands over her library card and signs me in as a guest. I admit we look odd or maybe suspicious, with both of us wearing tie-dyed t-shirts, she in a red and orange pattern and I in green and blue. Dada Zakiya reckons if we wear similar t-shirts, then I will not look like a beggar. Luckily, to the librarian we seem like two normally behaved students, and she allows us to enter.

"All right, here we are." Dada Zakiya shows me the way. "Now we can roam the library and be free with the books." She does a three-sixty spin. "Come on, let's get you lots of books." We zoom towards the children's book section.

I am in awe of the variety of books. I never imagined

seeing so many books all together in my life. Dada Zakiya tells me that in universities there are a hundred times more books. "What?" I scream. "You will read so much more, Dada?" I shake my head in disbelief. She giggles and then leads me towards the section of my interest. I pick many books from the shelves, properly organized in alphabetical order, and settle on the blue couch by the reading area against the window. Rain patters on the glass, like a symphony of African drums, and a chorus of frogs croaks outside in the mud puddles. One can almost dance to the music. The mood is perfect and the books are a gift from God, and so is Dada Zakiya. She lets me read by myself for a long time. I flip page after page, intrigued by photographs of different airplanes. It seems like one of the airplanes flew all the way to the moon. Must be a make-believe tale, like *Alice in Wonderland*, one of my favourite books. Dada Zakiya has read it to me at least three times and has promised to read it once more. I am lost in the books, with the words and the pictures. After a while, I check on Dada Zakiya reading a big people's book with plenty of writing. "A book without pictures?" I ask. "That looks difficult; it would put me to sleep. Is it hard?"

"Of course!" she nods. "I am reading French. Everything about French is hard."

"Why are you learning it then?" I ask seriously.

"It's a challenge. You learn English and I learn French," she says.

I sometimes do not understand Dada Zakiya's thinking. Why would she want to challenge herself? What would be the use of a doctor knowing French? But I dare not ask.

After a while she brings a book of her choice for me to read. She is happy with my progress and praises me. I take my exercise book and write TANK YU. She writes back THANK YOU.

I notice a couple of *Wahindi* girls sitting across from us on the red couch giving us a stare. Dada Zakiya moves closer towards me, placing the book in between her and my lap. I read to her as she moves her finger over the sentences.

"Shame! Shame!" says one of the girls.

"*Malaya*, whore," says the other.

I feel awkward and uneasy. I move slightly away from Dada Zakiya. The book slips off her lap and drops onto the floor. Dada Zakiya covers my ear with her palm and whispers, "Don't mind them. They don't know anything better." She picks up the book, clings to me and continues to move her finger under the words. Although I am uncomfortable with the situation, I continue to read, but my voice trembles. The girls look at each other in disgust and leave. "Good riddance." Dada Zakiya brushes her palms together. "Never be ashamed of our friendship. People talk. Who cares? I don't. Do you?" I shake my head but I am upset with the name-calling. Dada Zakiya deserves only praise, not insults.

"You, my friend, Master Juma, have earned lots of points today." She changes the subject and puts me at ease.

"Master? Points?" I ask, confused.

"Yes, master," she nods. "I may not need to move my finger over the words any longer. You read well without skipping the line." She pats my back. I join my palms in a prayer position and smile at her. "Come, follow me," she says. "I will show you the second floor. It's filled with special books."

The spiral stairs to the floating second floor give the illusion that they are reaching the sky. I imagine myself going beyond the sky and the clouds and meeting my angel. Mama could be there with God. I stand in the middle of the staircase with my mouth open and gaze at the skylight. "One day, Juma," Dada Zakiya says, as if she knows what I am imagining. She grabs my hand and walks me up the stairs. I sit on the floor while Dada Zakiya pulls out a thick book that reads *World Atlas* and settles next to me. When she opens the book, the drawings of our magical world appear in different shapes, sizes and colours. She points out where we live. "Imagine! We live in this country." She drags her finger to the other side of the map. "And I want to move here. This is where I will go to university and become a doctor."

"What is it called?" I ask.

"Canada," she says with such pride, as though she had been born there.

"Dada, but . . . but our countries are not connected."

"True. That is why I will have to take an airplane, cross the ocean and fly to the other side."

"Airplane! Lucky," I say. "But you are moving very far away. Please don't go. How will I survive without you? I don't want to be lost in my life."

"Hey!" She snaps her fingers. "I will be back to visit. I promise."

I borrow the book on airplanes and she borrows her *World Atlas* with her card. The librarian fills up my registration form. My own card will be ready for my next visit, and I can come back here on weekdays to look at more books all by myself.

At past midnight, the street quietens and I settle in the garage. I bunk myself as usual at the back of a car that is parked in the garage overnight. My thoughts wander around the *World Atlas* that Dada Zakiya showed me at the library earlier in the afternoon. I close my eyes and imagine crossing the ocean with Dada Zakiya to the other side.

We fly in the air and a big cloud comes over us. It picks us up and moves us farther and farther away from the city. There is no one to be seen, only Dada Zakiya and me.

The cloud slows down.

"Why are you slowing down?" Dada Zakiya asks.

"I cannot go any further," says the cloud.

"Why not? We need to be on the other side," I tell the cloud.

"Because only one can go to the other side and the other one has to return home," says the cloud.

Dada Zakiya and I cling to one another and refuse to part.

The cloud turns dense and dark. It gets wet and breaks into rain. We cannot hang onto the cloud anymore and we pour down with the rain. We drop in the middle of the ocean. A school of dolphins swims by and takes us deep down into the sea.

Dada Zakiya and I swim and see many colourful fish and coral reefs. The ocean allows us to live in their world.

Dada Zakiya sends a message to the cloud that she no longer wishes to go to the other side. I send a message to the cloud that I no longer wish to go back home. What a beautiful and free world this is.

I suddenly open my eyes and snap back to the lonely dark night. Dada Zakiya's voice echoes in my head. "I will be back to visit. I promise." This time, I close my eyes and sleep.

drive-in
november 1979

DADA ZAKIYA SUGGESTS I watch a film with her tonight. "My uncle is visiting from out of town, and he wants to take us to the drive-in cinema. Oh, I am so excited!" She jumps as she tells me. "I want you to experience this open theatre with me. It will be so much fun. A mega film *Suhaag* is playing this weekend. I just can't wait. My favourite Parveen Babi casts in the film."

"Are you crazy? Mama Fatima will never allow it," I say.

"Well, we have to be tricky then, don't we." She holds her chin. "Let me think." After a short pause, she says, "I got it!" and snaps her fingers. "Hamisi is preparing a picnic for us to take. I will come downstairs to the car to help him load. At that time, I will sneak you into the trunk at the back."

That sounds like a bad plan. "No, Dada, I will get caught."

"Don't be a pussycat."

"How?" I shake my head.

"Like lizards when they camouflage and you don't even see them. Once I was adjusting a picture frame at home and something moved. Hamisi tells me there are plenty of lizards in our home and we don't even know where. That's how. Now, be there, under the stairs at five in the evening."

"Okay, but I still think it's a bad idea," I say. "Besides, I don't know where you live."

"Come with me. I'll show you."

She whistles a faint tune as we walk towards central downtown where lots of *Wahindi* reside in their flats. The buildings are mostly five storeys high, with stores and restaurants and spice shops on the ground floor. Dada Zakiya lives on the third storey in a building across from *Darkhana*, Ismaili mosque. A huge *Muhindi* man sits at the entrance of the *Darkhana* talking to himself. I wonder if I look like him, peculiar, when I talk to myself. People pass by him; they either ignore him or laugh at him, but somehow I understand him. I observe a special glow in his eyes, sensing a truthful being. When I smile, he blinks and continues to talk to himself. Dada Zakiya waves at him. He continues to talk to himself. "You see all the badges he wears?" she says. "Each one has a story, but only he knows."

I think about Mama's *kanga* I carry, given by her father when she became a woman, the only possession left from her family. Her *kanga* has its own story too. With it wrapped around my tiny body after my birth, she proudly presented a grandson to her father. Later on, the *kanga* turned into a baby carrier, with me on her back while she worked at the *shamba*, farm, helping her father. She never spoke of my father. Whenever I asked, she told me that I was too little to understand and she would tell me one day. The drought killed my grandfather, while Mama with one-year-old me was forced to the city and a beggar she became. The *kanga* survived against all odds till her last day, carrying her ashes, ending her story. And now, the same *kanga* that I hug and put myself to sleep with every night tells my story, but only I know.

Dada Zakiya and I cross the road and walk through the alley smelling of trash. Egg shells, banana peels, chicken bones and other stuff, I do not know what, all mashed up and scattered to the side by the wall. We reach the back of the building of her flat. "So hide here." She points under the stairs. "I will come and get you. Now, remember to be quiet. We don't want mother to hear you. Do you know she has elephant ears? She can hear neighbours talking two flats across." She claps my hand and laughs loud enough for the residents going up the stairs to stare at us. I am still not sure about this plan at all. Dada Zakiya refuses to listen and insists on taking me to the cinema with her.

In the evening, I wait under the stairs. A man passes by with the picnic *kikapu*, basket. It has got to be Hamisi. About fifteen minutes later, Dada Zakiya comes to find me. She puts her finger to her lips and I follow her to the car parked on the street.

"*Ahsante*, Hamisi," she thanks him. Hamisi looks at both of us askance. Dada Zakiya signals him to leave, raising both her brows.

"He will tell Mama Fatima," I say. "I think I better go."

"No, he will not. Hamisi favours me all the time. He promised my grandmother at her deathbed that he would care for me. I come first." She speaks with a confidence that scares me. She settles me in the trunk. "Don't make any noise. When I open the trunk, you have to be ready to jump out. Understand?"

"Okay, Dada," I say with calmness, completely the opposite of how I feel.

I smell the food from the *kikapu* and am tempted to eat, but that would be stealing. The rusty base of the car has many holes and I see the road right through it. The car moves fast and the tarmac seems endless. We turn into a bumpy road and I hit my head on the side, but I dare not make any sound.

I hear conversation in the car and the songs playing. Mama Fatima grumbles about money and how hard she has to work. Dada Zakiya is mad. "Why don't you, for once, enjoy the moment?" she snaps at her mother. Uncle calms them down, and they have a more pleasant conversation.

After a long ride, the car comes to a stop. "We will be stopped for a while, until the ticket booth opens," Dada Zakiya says. Her uncle acknowledges her, although I think she is sending me the message. The aroma of food tortures my hunger, but I promise not to touch the *kikapu* at all. After some time, the car moves slowly and I hear a man asking for thirty-nine shillings for the price of the tickets. So much money, I think to myself; this could feed me for a whole month.

I jump out like a grasshopper when Dada Zakiya opens the trunk. The lady in the car parked behind points and tells her *bwana* about us. Dada Zakiya ignores them; she does not care. "As long as my mother doesn't find out, we are safe," she whispers. I walk to the other side and stand a couple of cars away while Dada Zakiya lets Mama Fatima know that she is going around looking for her friends. We cheer in amazement at our successful plan. We reach the last row of space at the back of the theatre by the high concrete wall where no cars are parked. We find a perfect spot next to the pole where the speakers hang. "I will go back to the car and tell Mother that I am with a friend. Munch munch time. I'll bring us the food and a blanket too," Dada Zakiya says. "Stay here and save our spot."

What a huge cinema, packed with countless cars and people! Six men in the row across from me place a mat in between two parked cars and joyfully play cards, drink beer and smoke. In the meantime, the women in their company empty the trunks of both cars and set up the food on a blanket on the hood. After their meal, all five women take off for a walk. I assume one of the six men may not have a woman. I eagerly wait for Dada Zakiya to bring my picnic treat.

The young group gathered next to me speak of a game of *antakshri*. Once they start playing, I figure out that each player begins the song with the sound that the previous player ended with. I watch and envy their fulfilled life. How privileged these youngsters are, I think to myself.

Dada Zakiya finally comes back. "Sorry, my friend. I was stuck with some boring relatives who came by to meet my uncle, and I had to eat with them." She lays down the mat for us to sit on and spreads the blanket on our laps. "To keep away the mosquito bites," she says. "Here, I brought you some food. Hamisi has made some *kebabs* and *bhajias*. And cold, cold Coca-Cola, of course, the best drink ever." Dada Zakiya eats her cake and saves me a piece.

"Slow down, Juma. Don't gobble it. You will get a tummy ache."

"I am hungry. I am *so* hungry." I still gobble it down.

"Satisfied?" she asks when I finish.

"Yes! *Ahsante*," I lie to her, because I am still hungry. But I forget my hunger when the girl in the group is stuck during her turn to sing. She cannot think of any song that starts with the sound Y.

"*You can dance, you can jive, having the time of your life . . . dig in the dancing queen . . .*" Dada Zakiya sings.

My mouth falls open when I hear her powerful projected voice. The group claps in amazement. They all get up and circle around us. We join the game. I sing Kiswahili songs, some Mama used to sing to me and many I hear from the bar, while most of them sing Hindi songs. We laugh and share jokes. What a life! If I could freeze the moment—this would be it.

It gets dark and the picture starts. My first film experience, the story comes alive on the huge screen, all the way from the front of the theatre with the sound right next to me. This is so magical. Now I understand why everyone hangs around by the theatre to buy tickets at triple the price on the black market when the house is full. Dada Zakiya promises to take me to the city theatres one day, too.

During the interval, Dada Zakiya and I stretch and walk a couple of rows. We discuss the story and predict the next half of the film. We have different opinions, so let's see what happens. In the cafeteria, she buys us some chips and soda, and we settle back in our spot, eager to watch the next half of the film.

"Thank you, Dada, for allowing me to share this joyous moment with you," I say.

"For you, my friend, the moon," she says.

~

Next morning, Dada Zakiya, with her sleepy eyes, yawn-
ing, in her pyjamas, hair all messed up, lets me out of the
trunk. I laugh at her state. She rubs my head and gives me
a thick slice of bread and a banana. "Have a great Sunday.
Now I will go back to sleep. See you next week." She
drags her feet as she goes back to her home.

I smile to myself and walk the streets. I think of the
film and the rich, colourful, traditional stick dance scene.
The beautiful song rings in my ears. I also think about the
group of youngsters who sang terribly and the gifted voice
of Dada Zakiya. Furthermore, I think about the dilemma
of trying to sneak back into the trunk, which almost got
us both into trouble. But it all ended well, and tonight I
will tell the night ladies of my film expedition, a risky
adventure, no doubt. However, as Dada Zakiya says, life
is an adventure, and if you don't take a chance, you miss
out on the opportunity.

I pass by a *maskini* boy and his mother, lying on the
cardboard by the corner alley, just waking up. I wonder
how long they will be safe. Then I question myself: What
if she dies? Please, God, no, not yet, he is too young to be
alone, I pray for him. I offer them the bread and banana.
After all, I had my share of food last night; let this morning be their turn. The boy grabs it from my hand without
hesitation. I carry on with the walk, the smile and the
thought of the film.

prayers
may 1980

"DADA, WATCH OUT!" I scream and press my hands over my head. She does not respond even though the driver of the car passing by honks and squeals the brakes. The screech draws everyone's attention but hers. "Are you crazy? You almost got killed!" She looks at me with her red, saggy eyes, not knowing what just happened. "Is everything all right, Dada?" I ask, considering she is normally alert and sharp.

She sighs and blinks several times. "I haven't slept well."

"Eat these chillies and be a true *Muhindi* friend," she dared me once. I took a tiny bite of the long green chilly. "A true *Muhindi* friend . . . a true *Muhindi* friend," I said, pretending it was not hot at all. Then I took another tiny bite and teased her more. "Don't be a show-off, you cannot pretend," she laughed. "Eyes always say the truth," and she brushed the tears off my face.

Similarly today, her eyes cannot hide the truth from me. She sits sluggishly next to me while I read her my homework. I skip a line on purpose and she does not even notice. I throw my exercise book on the ground and seek the truth. "All right, what is it?"

"Sorry! Juma, I am not focused today. Let's take a day off studying." She gets up and makes to leave.

"Don't go. Let me take you to a special spot and show you something," I say. Deep in her own thoughts, she follows me.

We come across a *madafu*, coconut, vendor at the corner of the street, comfortably located under the awning of the shop window. He speaks as we pass. "Sweet and cooling, special price." I stop and ask him to choose the sweetest one for Dada Zakiya. The vendor knocks a few coconut shells with his knuckles. "Ahh! This one sounds sweet and soft," and he breaks it with a small tarnished knife. Dada Zakiya takes the coconut, drinks up the juice and hands it back to the vendor. She remains silent while the vendor scoops soft meat with a piece of scrap wood. She slurps the fruit and sticks her hand into the shell to scrape off the last bit with her fingers. "Six shillings," the vendor says and reaches out his palm.

Dada Zakiya does not look at the vendor or me, her mind occupied elsewhere. I empty all the coins from my pocket and count as I pay the vendor: five cents, ten, sixty, sixty-five, seventy, eighty, eighty-five . . .

The frustrated vendor raises his voice. "*Haraka*, hurry up." Dada Zakiya takes ten shillings from her pocket, dumps it on his palm and walks away. Relieved, I grab my eighty-five cents back from the vendor and get Dada Zakiya's change too. I hand her four shillings but she shakes her head no. With pleasure, I put the coins in my pocket.

I take Dada Zakiya to the bay by the ferry berth. We walk down towards the calm beach. The tide is low and the sun shines over the ocean, creating a sparkling effect. Dada Zakiya's shrugged shoulders drop when she feels the energy of the ocean air. A young man passes by with three cows. Dada Zakiya startles at first. "Is he serious?" She laughs.

It feels good to hear her laugh. "Have you not seen cows before?" I ask.

"Not on the beach."

"He is probably a local milk vendor, going back home," I say.

"Thank you for bringing me here. I have never been on this side of the beach."

"It's a ferry berth and the fishermen's spot." I wave at the fishermen coming ashore in their dhows with a fresh catch to take to the fish market. The seagulls circle anxiously and lose interest in the anchored dhows that belong to the fishermen from the morning catch. "Come follow me. I will show you the ferry," I say, and we walk towards the berth up to the end of the barge. I tell her about the dwellings across the water. "I will build my own hut one day and have a home there."

"On that small island?" She points her finger in that direction. "I never thought there would be homes there. Wow! It must be beautiful."

"So I hear, so I hear," I say. She smiles at me, allowing me to dream.

I show her the public tap where Mama and I used to wash ourselves. Dada Zakiya turns the tap. "This would take hours to wash up." The low flow shocks her.

"I know. That is why I use the public shower by the clock tower every Saturday morning before your visit. But it costs me."

"Oh Juma!" she sighs. "I didn't know that you went through so much trouble. And why were you paying for *madafu*?"

"I want you to be happy, Dada," I say. "Why are you so sad today?"

"Today is nine years since my father died. My mother will have a special prayer ceremony for him tonight. For food offering, she's asked Hamisi to cook fried *samaki*, fish, and potatoes, my father's favourite dish." This time she lets her tears release. "What is the point? He is dead." She covers her face with both hands.

I pat her back and take her down by the beach one more time, closer to the shore. I scoop water in my palm and pour it back into the ocean. "This is where I let

Mama's ashes free," I say. I hold her hand and ask her to pray with me. She acknowledges with a tight grip. We stare at the endless ocean and I pray. "Mama, my angel, this is my sister, Dada Zakiya. Tell her father that she takes good care of me. Her family is sending him some fish and potatoes tonight. Ask him to share the feast with you. I am very sure he is as kind as she is. Now you are not alone." Dada Zakiya nods when I look at her. "Also thank Hamisi for cooking up such a wonderful meal for my mama and your father."

She gives me a hug. "Thank you. Now I understand."

We walk back to the town in silence.

I stand at the foot of the stairs below Dada Zakiya's flat and wait for her. A young boy and girl holding hands, trying to kiss each other, are not happy to see me interrupt their meeting. They give me a stare. I ignore them. Thank heavens Dada Zakiya arrives soon. She hands me a small bowl wrapped in a newspaper.

"What is it?" I ask.

"Take it to your street and enjoy it," she says. We both glance at the young couple and chuckle. They do not seem amused. Halfway up the stairs, Dada Zakiya turns back and shouts, "You are my best friend, Juma," and waves goodbye.

"*Ahsante*, Dada," I whisper to myself.

I settle in a nice shady place under a tree by the park

and remove the newspaper covering the bowl, and discover a delicious fried fish and potatoes cooked in *masala*. "Look, Mama, I get some too," I tell my angel. The aroma of strong spice waters my mouth. I dig my fingers into the bowl, scoop the food and take the first bite. Wow! Now, that is spicy; there is a lot of heat in it. I stick my tongue out and air it with my hand, then continue to eat. What a talented cook Hamisi is.

Dada Zakiya has told me about Hamisi. He has been working for her family since her father and mother were married. Dada Zakiya's grandmother taught him to cook. After her grandmother died, Hamisi took over the kitchen. He has been preparing their meals daily, just like this fish and potatoes, the best meal I have had in a long time. I lick the bowl clean and admire the lovely flowery designs around the rim. The initials J.K. painted with bright red nail polish on the bottom of the bowl must belong to Dada Zakiya's father. Not knowing his full name, I shall call him Baba JK.

I sit by the lamppost next to the restaurant, place Baba JK's bowl beside me, and thank him for a truly blessed day. By the end of the evening, many coins have clinked into the bowl. In my exercise book, I write down J.K. and I think about Mama. I remember the nurse telling me to find out her name once she feels better. I never got a chance to do so, but today I will give *Mama yangu* a name.

I write:

J.K.

J. FOR JULIANA

K. FOR KIPANGA

MY MATHERS NAME IS JULIANA KIPANGA

MY NAME IS JUMA KIPANGA

WOT IS YOR FATHER NAME DADA ZAKIYA?

Today I have a name. I finally have a name. I will ask
Dada Zakiya to show me how to write *kipanga*, falcon, in
English, and one day I will be flying high and free just
like it.

choices
july 1980

FOR THE PAST two months, ever since I showed Dada Zakiya the ferry berth, we have been coming here every Saturday after my lessons. "I feel a great deal of energy and joy today," Dada Zakiya says while watching the stillness of the ocean. "So much *shanti*." *Shanti* for sure, I think to myself, especially with the fishermen away at the market, the ferry workers fast asleep and even the seagulls missing from the sky. Not even a wind, it is an exceptionally quiet afternoon. "Why does it feel so different?" she asks.

"Because the happy souls are near us today," I say, staring straight ahead at the ocean.

"Do you think they can hear us?" she asks. I nod. She joins her palms in a prayer position. "Thank you to the great souls. Thank you to the fishermen for our daily meal. Most of all, thank you to the wonders of the ocean. I will always be part of you, anywhere I go. Amen." She tells me that even when she moves away, she will speak to the happy souls, to her father and Mama from the other side of the ocean. "In the next two years, *Inshallah*, if God wills." She sighs as though her heart has filled with happiness and sorrow at the same time.

All of a sudden, the ocean seems dull and lifeless as though the happy souls also heard Dada Zakiya's future planning and do not wish her to go. I sulk and look away. "Look at me, Juma, please look at me," she says in her sweet tone.

"Find me a job, I must work," I say. "I must move into my own hut. I am fed up with the streets, the begging, smelling the bar every night. And . . . and the music, the dark . . ."

"Juma," Dada Zakiya interrupts. I stay quiet. She removes her sunglasses and looks right into my eyes. Her brown eyes shine as the pupils shrink into a tiny sparkle. She rubs both my hands with her soft-as-cotton-wool hands to soothe me. "You've been studying for almost two years and the results are phenomenal. Remember where you were and where you are. Wait for another two and you will be ready."

"What?" I let go of her hand. "That is too long. You told me two years. Now you are saying another two. No, I can't wait. What if you leave the country before that? Then what?" I dig my foot into the sand and kick it.

"I promise I will find you work before I go. Have faith in me." She grabs hold of my hands again. The softness of her touch calms me slightly while she grips my rough and cracked palm. "Juma, you need to grow. You have to be taller."

"I look fine, I am tall enough," I say like the stubborn and spoilt *Wahindi* children I have witnessed many times. How stupid they seem, but then I am desperate.

"I know it is frustrating," she says. "I understand you want to have a decent life, but please be patient. I am frustrated too. The immigration papers are taking so long, and yet I am being patient, aren't I?"

I nod reluctantly, and she smiles at me. "Thank you," she says. "Now be patient, okay?"

That is easy for her to say. She has a home to go to at the end of the day. She has food on the table and a comfortable bed to sleep on. God has been nice to her.

Later in the evening, I find a charcoal at the back of the restaurant by the barbeque waste and mark my height on the wall behind the building to keep track of my growth. I refuse to wait another two years. I must use all the tricks to grow faster and convince Dada Zakiya to get me out of my misery at the earliest, however hopeless it seems for now. Dada Zakiya tells me I should not let anyone step over my legs or else I will never grow tall. She also suggests I jump one hundred times every night, but for that I need energy, and for that I need food.

I sit next to the restaurant cross-legged, ready to beg. The glamorous night ladies gather for their business. I receive my first coin of the evening from one of their male customers. The night lady winks at me. Arm in arm, the couple walk into the bar, passing by a group of people standing by the entrance in a circle speaking to one another as though they were debating. I wonder what they are speaking about. Even if I went closer, it would be impossible to hear them, with the loud music blasting on the street. The restaurant customers' chatter, and the cling and clang of utensils, frustrate me. The smell of deep fried oil is overwhelming. I wait in anticipation for fate to be on my side with a generous meal. I just need one miracle.

My attention is drawn to a burgundy Escort passing by the street for the third time, rattling as though it will fall apart any minute; the entire family in the car may need to take a taxi home. The two young girls in the car stick their heads out the window and make silly sounds. The *bwana*, their father (I assume), decides to take a spot in front of the closed garage gate, which has enough space to fit a small car, although it is a no parking area. He steps out and asks his wife and the girls to stay in the car, and goes into the restaurant. The fidgety girls seem to annoy their mother. "Quiet, both of you!" says the impatient mother. Just then, a police car passes by. It stops and two policemen get out to check the lady in the car.

"Where is the driver?" one of the policemen asks.

"He is inside getting takeout dinner," says the lady. "We will leave right away."

"This is a no parking area. Go get him." The policeman is rude.

The girls slam the door and run into the restaurant to call their father. The furious *bwana* screams and has an argument with the police. "What the heck are you hassling my family for? Just give us the ticket and get out of here." He is very angry. The policemen ask him to pay them five hundred shillings and they will call it a day. "Just give me the ticket. I will come to the police station and pay my dues. I am not paying you bloody bastards a penny." The *bwana* is ridiculously mad, shouting and creating a scene.

"You come to the police station with us right away!" One of the policemen takes out a set of handcuffs.

"Call Parvez Uncle and ask him to come to the station to get me," the *bwana* tells his wife. "I will not pay these people any money."

The policemen throw the *bwana* roughly into their jeep and take him away. The girls cry and the lady tries to calm them down. She takes them inside the restaurant to make a phone call. People gather outside from the restaurant and chatter among themselves. "Why did he just not pay them?" a man from the crowd says. "They would have settled for one hundred, if he had bargained. How irresponsible of him to leave his wife and children stranded at night." Someone else agrees: "Now he will have to pay triple the amount to get released from the station." Everyone has their own opinion, yet no one helps the lady and her girls. In a short while, two men arrive in a car. The lady and her girls are driven off in the *bwana's* car by one of the men while the other man heads to the station in his car. He must be Parvez Uncle.

The crowd clears and everyone goes back to minding their own business. The night ladies who had disappeared come back. "For a minute I thought they had come to arrest us," I overhear one night lady telling the other.

"I was ready to give them a good time with the glow-in-the-dark condoms that the *Muzungu* tourist left for me," the other night lady says. They give a high clap to each other and laugh. Dodging the police takes talent, and the night ladies have mastered how.

I sigh and am relieved that the commotion is over so the passersby can pay attention to me, and once again I take my spot. Eventually, someone hands me some food from the restaurant wrapped in a newspaper. I think of the lady and her girls while I eat. How happy they looked, and now they probably do not have food for the evening. I agree with the crowd: it was the father's fault. He should have paid the money to the policemen, got his food and gone home.

After a while, I hear a smart-looking young man in a clean white shirt and fancy trousers having a conversation with one of the night ladies. His voice sounds so familiar that I go and stand next to him. "Hey! Do you have a problem, brother?" he exclaims and pushes me towards the pole.

"Samuel?" I question softly, unsure that he would remember me. I have not seen him since my farewell to Mama.

"Juma! For heaven's sake, is this you? What are you doing here?" He flaps his hands up towards the sky. "Come on." He pokes me. "Don't tell me this is your new street to beg." The night lady asks if he is bothering me. "*Nini?* What?" Samuel laughs. "Seems like . . ." and he laughs louder. "Is she your bodyguard?" he teases me.

I stand in front of Samuel, stunned. I do not utter a word and yet so many questions go through my thoughts. This is so unexpected. Gosh! I had not realized until now that I actually missed him. Samuel, my friend, whom I have admired since I was little and once dreamt to be like. Look at him. Wow! Look at him, smelling of *Muzungu* cologne. Maybe I still dream to be like him. This peculiar feeling jolts my body and I stand stiff as a rock, in a state of shock.

"You have grown taller. My god, look at you," Samuel says. "Gosh, you look like shit."

"Do you know him?" the night lady asks me.

"Yes, he is my lost brother," I say softly, my voice shaking as though I am unsure of how he is going to react.

"Yes, that's right, my lost brother," Samuel repeats with a nod. He takes the night lady a few steps away and they talk for a while. He gives me a sign to follow him, and the three of us go upstairs to the motel.

How comforting and pleasant it feels when we step into the air-conditioned room, despite the cool climate. The size of the huge bed in the middle of the room astonishes me. Goodness me, I never knew Samuel could afford this too. I have been a bloody fool all along.

"Sit down, brother." Samuel jumps on the bed. "Now we have found each other, no more losing you again, understand?" He gets up, comes closer to me and sniffs my t-shirt. "Or maybe . . . I mean, why don't you go and take a bath? Smell a bit better and then we can spend time together tonight." He walks me to the bathroom.

I close the door and undress. I remember the picture book Dada Zakiya read to me once about the bear in the bathtub who scrubbed himself with a brush as he sang. I soak in the tub and pretend to be the bear. I scrub my feet and my slippers with a small towel and sing. The soap smells like the jasmine flower, just like the ones dangling on *Wahindi* ladies' hair. The soap reads LUX on it, and I wonder if that is short for luxury. Well, it surely feels like it.

Samuel opens the door and asks me to hurry up. He hands me a toothbrush and salt. "Scrub your teeth until you do not see a sign of yellow colour." Samuel is sarcastic as always but I do not mind; at least he shows he cares.

"Where are you taking my clothes?" I ask him when he

picks them up and almost leaves the bathroom with them.

"These are not clothes, they are rags. I am going to throw them out." He holds them far away from his face in disgust.

"No! What will I wear? My t-shirt is new. Dada Zakiya gave it to me."

"This shitty t-shirt is new?" He laughs when I nod. "Okay, we will keep the t-shirt. Now, hurry up. And who is Dada Zakiya?"

"She comes to this street in the daytime, and she is my friend."

"A beggar?" he asks.

"She is Mama Fatima's daughter. Mama Fatima owns the hairdressing salon downstairs. Dada Zakiya teaches me how to read and write."

Samuel drops the clothes back on the floor, sits at the edge of the tub and splashes water on my face. "What good is that going to do you?" he asks. "I cannot believe that you still waste time on things that are not important. But don't you worry, brother. I am here and we will never part again. Now hurry up." He picks up the clothes and leaves.

With a towel wrapped around my waist, I come out of the bathroom. "Where are my clothes?" I ask Samuel. Samuel throws my t-shirt back to me. "What about my shorts?"

Samuel stomps closer to me and pulls off my towel. I stand there naked, waist down. The night lady laughs at me. Samuel laughs as well and jumps on the bed next to the lady. I feel humiliated. I cup my palm and cover my privates. The lady pulls out a men's underwear from her purse and hands it to me. "It's big but we can always mend it with a knot. I stole it from one of my foreign customers."

"Okay, this will do for the night. Come here on this nice comfortable bed." Samuel hits the mattress.

I sit on the bed and feel the softness of the mattress. Yes, comfortable *kabisa*, for sure. I think of Mama and feel grateful that she got a chance to sleep on a bed at least once in her lifetime. Tonight is my turn.

The night lady opens a bottle of beer and offers me a sip. I am thrilled. I grab it from her hand. The first sip is bitter. I make a disapproving face and grimace, yet I take another sip. Samuel offers me a cigarette. I cough when I inhale. Samuel and the night lady seem quite entertained by me; they laugh a lot. After a few puffs, I get better. I inhale more and drink more. I do not remember when I fall asleep.

The next morning, I wake up beside the night lady, who is sleeping sideways facing me. One of her huge breasts presses against the mattress, and the other one falls on top of it. I want to touch her but shy away, fearing that she may wake up. Samuel, sleeping on the other side, clings to her with his hands on her bare body. I admire his strong physique and feel ashamed of my skinny and ugly body.

Samuel wakes up. "You had a good sleep?" he asks.

I nod and smile. "I do not remember when I last slept so well."

"Maybe never," he reminds me. "So would you like to have a good life?" He gets up from the bed and puts on his trousers.

"You still haven't given up on me, have you?" I stand next to him.

"Never." He stretches his arm to shake my hand. "I will now tell you all about a job we can do together. It's time we did it, yeah?"

"All right, let's do it." Fate has brought us together again. This must be my destiny. Besides, I would like to drink Pilsner, sleep in this comfortable bed and smoke 555 every day.

Yes, now I am ready to be Samuel's partner. Except on Saturdays, I will pretend to be a *maskini* and spend time with Dada Zakiya while learning to read and write.

market
july 1980

SAMUEL AND I pass the interview with the Keshavji brothers. Here we are, the two of us, in this hungry city where
we are about to make our dreams happen. Jumping for
joy, clapping one another's hands and making sounds of
victory with our tongues, we make men and women, and
also children, on the streets envy us. They stare, wondering about our celebration. I want to hug them and tell
them that I have a job that will make me amongst the rich
ones, a job that Samuel has believed in since I was little,
where I do not need to grow up or grow taller—I am
perfect the way I am. We could have done this a long
time ago if Mama had not stopped me. Although part of
me worries, I hope I am not making a mistake. When I
reason with myself that it is the right decision, Mama gets
on my conscience. I tell her that I am sorry but I have to

do this; after all, I do not want to die helpless like she did.

I hug Mama's *kanga* and my books in an absolute thrill and get ready for my big move with Samuel. For the first time, today I will have a home, a moment I have dreamt of ever since I can remember. I cannot believe that I am not a *maskini* anymore. Mama's voice haunts me: "You are a *mwizi*, a *mwizi*, a *mwizi*." I press my palms against my ears and ask her to go away.

Samuel points at a thin, tall woman standing by the entrance to the ferry, wearing a clean dress and a yellow patterned *kanga* wrapped around her waist. "Her name is Esta. She lives next to my hut. If she asks, just tell her you are my lost brother."

"You are my family now anyway," I say.

Next to her stands a young boy, probably seven years old, who appears as clean as Esta. "That little boy with her is Emanuel, her son. He is sneaky and asks a lot of questions, so be careful." The boy looks right at us as though he has figured out that we are talking about him. He smiles at Samuel. Samuel acknowledges him with a nod. "See, I told you. He is already stirring up stories and questions to ask."

"He is a child. Why would I tell him anything?" I say.

"*Haya, lakini*, okay, as long as you know. Be careful. Otherwise, people talk and then the police will find out and we are doomed. They all think I have a job in town, so let's keep it that way."

"I understand," I say.

We board the ferry. Although it seems chaotic, everyone knows their order and no one struggles to fit into the packed ferry. Women take their spots on the benches by the sides and relax with their babies and children on their laps. Most of the people with bicycles settle in the front. The rest of us stand behind them. Families with children, men and their women, men alone, women alone—everyone looks relieved, happy or relaxed because they are heading home, to the comfort of their own living space. And the best part is, so am I. Everything feels perfect. The breeze feels perfect too, fresher and cleaner, whatever the reason. We pass the fishermen sailing in their dhows, heading towards home. They wave at us as they sing, enjoying their journey at the end of the day. "I suppose they had a good business today," I say.

"They struggle too," Samuel says, "but at the end of the day they have a fish to take home for dinner. Everyone envies the fishermen. But not me, no, no, no, no way. I have a good meal every day too, and so will you."

This could be the best thing I have heard in a long time. A slight wind blows on my face when we step out of the ferry. I take a deep breath and inhale the fresh air. The shore is different. Instead of seaweed, there are plenty of coloured shells of different sizes all over. The grit of sand feels coarser when it gets in between my toes. We walk overland for almost fifteen minutes.

"You can bring a bucket of water and use any of these

facilities for your daily washing. The last three facilities have holes in them for the long visit to the queen." Samuel laughs and points at the row of outhouses as we approach the residential side. "Some of the men have houseboy jobs in the city. Beware of them when they visit the facilities. My god, I think they are fed too much *dengu*, lentil." He laughs again. "What a disgusting job, I mean cleaning people's homes all day."

I say nothing. Best thing is to nod and agree, even though I do not find anything disgusting about that job.

"Here we are, brother, my palace. *Karibu*, welcome," he says with pride when we reach his hut—a solid mud house with bricks in between the walls and sturdy, weaved sticks on the roof, topped with dried grass that makes it stronger and rainproof. We walk through the draped mosquito net at the entrance. Samuel goes directly to the cooking area at the far corner of the room and turns on the two lanterns that hang on each side of the kerosene stove. Beside the stove stands a wooden shelf, neatly stocked with condiments in Coca-Cola bottles, salt and spices, utensils and dishes. Next to it a banana-leaf weaved *kikapu*, basket, filled with corn flour has been placed on the ground. I never expected Samuel to be this neat and organized. He pulls a small stool in front of the stove. "Let me cook up a special meal for you today, brother," he says, signalling me to sit next to him.

I sit on the sisal mat, not believing my luck, and secretly pinch myself. Samuel turns on the transistor radio. He fiddles with the knob until the station is clear. He picks up a pot and plays the same *ngoma* beat that is airing on the radio. I stand up and swirl my body into a dance till the music is over. Then he throws spinach and beef into the pot to make soup. I settle back on the sisal mat and watch him cook. The aroma of boiling meat marks the beginning of my good days. Samuel serves us *ugali*, corn meal, and soup in shiny tin bowls. He cuts a banana into thin slices and gives me half of it. Afterwards, Samuel prepares hot and delicious *uji*, cream of wheat, and we nibble on peanuts while discussing our new job and how to split our earnings.

"I will calculate your cost of living and give you your share from the Keshavji brothers accordingly, if that is fine with you," Samuel says.

"Whatever you think is fair, I trust you. Thank you for welcoming me to your home."

"Yes, yes. I better remember you ate a serving of beef, spinach, *ugali*, slices of banana, a handful of peanuts, and drank *uji*."

"I can write it down. Dada Zakiya has taught me how to write."

"Yeah, right, as if you can," Samuel says and laughs sarcastically. I pull out my exercise book and a pencil and write down my expenses on the last page. For a moment he stares at the book in disbelief, and then grabs it from my hand to examine my writing. Without a word, he drops the book on the ground and walks to the other side that splits off into a bedroom.

"You see, I will not only be a rich beggar but also a smart beggar." This time I take the liberty of teasing him as I follow him to the bedroom, which is spacious enough to fit a mattress and a small trunk.

He picks up one of the pillows and throws it to me. "This is your side to sleep. Come on, get comfortable," and he opens the mosquito net tied to the ceiling and spreads it around the mattress. "I will show you my trunk of clothes tomorrow. Later on, you can have your own trunk when you earn. Imagine, you will be able to buy cologne and shoes and so much more."

Plenty has happened in a day—all my dreams are to come true. I excuse myself and walk outside into the pitch-dark, quiet space to absorb it all in silence. I look up at the stars. One in particular, the brightest of all, smiles back at me. That must be my lucky star, I think. "Thank you for being on my side, for once," I say, and go back inside the hut. Samuel is knocked out, fast asleep and snoring. I tuck myself on the soft mattress with my books and Mama's *kanga* next to me, and fall asleep as well.

I beg next to the soda stand at the peak hours of midday by the *sokoni*, market. A short *Muhindi* woman drops a coin into my palm. Her house worker walks behind her carrying a *kikapu* for the vegetables and fruits she may purchase at the market. "Shame on you, so young and begging. Get a job," he says to me. *This is my job, you bloody idiot*, I wish to tell him. I pretend to be a beggar and wait for a perfect opportunity to sell dollars at black market exchange. The Keshavji brothers are pleased with Samuel and me. We have done good business in the first three months. Samuel stands at the other end of the *sokoni* doing his surveillance, making sure no one suspects us. One man walks out of the market stall empty-handed, staring at me as though he is waiting for the right moment to approach me. But he purchases a cold soda instead and drinks it in one gulp, non-stop, until the bottle is empty, and goes on with his day. Samuel looks at me. I shake my head, and he knows that no one has come along for business, which is odd, considering that the soda man is relatively busy selling illegal goods—Colgate, almonds, chocolates, jeans and a lot more—although he makes the customers buy a bottle of soda first. The soda man and I nod and glance at each other all day in silent understanding: *I stay out of your business and you stay out of mine.* In fact, a lot of action takes place here, and everyone stays away from each other's business.

For instance, yesterday a *Muhindi* lady parked her car behind the *banda*, shed, away from public view. As soon as she walked into the *sokoni*, four boys removed the tires from her car. No one interfered with their business. When the lady returned, she realized her stupidity. All four boys stood next to her and watched her with a serious look, apparently as surprised as she was. She burst into laughter when she saw their expression. "All right!" she said. "Would you boys by any chance know if anyone is selling tires in this area?"

"This is your lucky day, Mama. There is a storekeeper behind the soda stand who has four tires at one hundred shillings each, *bas*," one of the boys said.

She bargained till they agreed on fifty shillings for each tire, provided they fit them back for her. The boys made their fifty each within an hour. Brilliant, absolutely brilliant, I thought to myself. Samuel had told me that this place is guaranteed to make you successful if you play your cards right.

By the end of the day, Samuel and I have made progress and sold almost all the dollars. We close our shift and go to the Keshavji brothers to hand them their money. The younger brother counts at least three times before paying us our commission. Samuel pockets our earnings. "We'll calculate at home," he says.

The Keshavji brothers pay us one shilling each for every dollar we exchange for them. At first, I was confused about how the system worked. What did it all mean? Where did the dollars come from? Why don't people go to the bank? "If we went to the bank, we would get seven shillings for an official one dollar. But guess what, brother?" Samuel says. "Our stupid bank does not have dollars because they are poor."

"I don't understand, nothing makes sense," I say.

"You see, brother, it is simple. We sell one dollar for thirty shillings, the Keshavji brothers give us two shillings, and they are left with twenty-eight. Now, that is a lot more than the official rate of seven shillings. No wonder the Keshavji brothers are bloody rich.

"But do not ask me how and where they get the money. All I know is that people are desperate to get dollars. Keshavjis know how to, and if you and I work hard, then our commissions will increase in time. Everyone wins."

Later in the evening, Samuel sits on the sisal mat next to me while I am on the stool preparing our meal, one of the many pleasures of having a home. The *maharagwe*, kidney beans, are cooking. I stir the *ugali* to a paste-like consistency. Samuel pops a bottle of beer for himself. I refuse such expense, and instead I pour a glass of boiled water for myself. "How about we settle my earnings after our meal?" I ask Samuel. "I want to keep my own cash I have earned."

"I doubt if there is anything left for you. Anyway, not today. We will calculate some other day." Samuel takes a sip of his beer and changes the subject. He is always dodging settling my commissions. Every so often, he adds some unreasonable expense to decrease my amount. For instance, last week he asked me to subtract five shillings. When I wanted to know the reason, he said he had worked on an exchange by himself while I was at the back taking a pee, as if he never goes to the back to take a leak. Reasoning with him is impossible; he comes up with excuses and shuts me up. Once again, with disappointment, I write down the commission I earned today and my share of the food I had with him this evening, and of course the hamburger and chips we bought at Wimpy, which was ridiculously expensive. We could have bought a full plate of rice and a piece of chicken at half the price from Jena Bai. Samuel wastes money. If only he gave me my share, then I could make my own choices.

On Friday, Samuel asks me to join him for an exciting time with the night ladies. I let him go ahead to enjoy his luxuries by himself while I head back home. I do not want to spend money on night ladies and beer. Last time, it cost me too much. "Enjoy life," Samuel had said. "It is your first time, so I have made a good deal with the beauty queen of this street."

It was a bad deal. Before I knew it, everything was over, and the night lady charged a lot. Samuel had a good time with her and I had to pay half. That wasn't fair at all. Samuel and I stayed in the room all night and drank beer. He kept spending and spending. I tried to remember my share but I couldn't, and he made me write a big amount in my exercise book. That was the first and last time I joined him for such luxuries. Dada Zakiya was worried about me when I didn't show up the next day for my studies. I do not even remember what excuse I made.

Lately, I have been lying to Dada Zakiya a lot. She is a bit suspicious of me. "Are you up to something I should know about?" she asks.

"No, Dada," I say, adding another lie that I feel horrible about.

Samuel does not understand why I bother to meet her on Saturdays. But then he wouldn't, would he.

I am glad he stays behind with the night ladies tonight. I am happy to be alone in the hut. I place a lantern next to me and read a book borrowed from the library. I jot down the words that I do not understand in my exercise book for Dada Zakiya to teach me. My eyes droop; I take Mama's *kanga* and wrap it around myself before I switch the lantern off. Sleeping in the comfort of a soft mattress—secured with the mosquito net—I send my thanks to my lucky, bright star. Good night and sweet dreams, I say to myself.

escape
january 1981

DURING THE BEGINNING of the year, the heat continues to bring many customers to the soda stand. Samuel and I get more chances to do the exchange in this bustle. One of our regular customers, Mansoor, slowly passes by Samuel in his car to purchase the dollars for his son, who lives out of the country. Samuel points at the parking spot to signal Mansoor to meet him there. They have a much longer discussion than usual. Then Samuel rushes to me and asks for more money. "He wants to purchase more than he normally does. I am sixty dollars short. Give me two hundred so I have enough for the day." I sneakily give him two stacks of one hundred dollar bills in various denominations finely folded together.

I remember the first time Mansoor purchased the dollars; he asked if we knew anyone who was travelling out of the country so he could arrange to send the money with them to his son. Samuel mentioned this to the Keshavji brothers. Later on that week, Mansoor visited the Keshavji brothers, an arrangement was made between them and the money got delivered to his son. Since then, he has been a regular buyer. He is a good father, and I hope his son appreciates how lucky he is.

Later in the afternoon, a fat *Muhindi* man shows up and leans on the side of the soda stand. The circles of perspiration around his armpits have left stains on his white shirt. Although the sweat drenches his underarms, he does not purchase a cold drink or take the shady spot. I gaze at him curiously. He clears his throat and acknowledges me by raising his brows. I realize *kumbe*, lo, he may be a potential buyer. I nod at him discreetly and he comes closer to me, takes a coin from his pocket and reaches for my palm. Instead, I show him a dollar. "You can give me thirty shillings and take the dollar, sir," I close my palm and go back to my beggar routine. He goes to the stand and buys me a soda. Samuel stands next to the tree across from me and I give him a "go" signal. I take the soda and leave. Samuel approaches the *Muhindi* man to negotiate the exchange. I wait at the other side and sip on the cold drink. At that very moment, a policeman walks out from the back of the *sokoni* and takes hold of me.

"Samuel!" I scream.

Samuel attempts to run away when he hears me, but the *Muhindi* man grabs him. He twists Samuel's hand

and pulls him towards a car. Samuel resists and tries to get away, but a hard punch follows. A crowd gathers. Some ladies panic, drop their *kikapus*, run to their cars and drive away. Samuel and I are both thrown against the car and handcuffed. The policeman is rough; he kicks me and forces me into the car. Samuel continues to resist the *Muhindi* man, who loses his patience. He throws another punch right on Samuel's nose, this time *much* harder, and shoves him next to me in the back of the car. Even though Samuel's nose bleeds, he does not show pain or fear. I am so scared. I don't want to go to jail.

"You can have ten dollars each and let us go," Samuel says to them.

"Now, why would I want to make ten dollars out of you when you will tell us who is the mastermind behind this operation and we can make thousands from them?" the *Muhindi* man says.

I am terrified. "I am sorry, I am sorry, please let me go."

"Shut up, you shut up," Samuel shouts at me and tells me not to say anything. He whispers to me that the Keshavji brothers will send someone to get us out of jail and free us if we keep their names out of it.

But we are not taken to the jail. Instead, we arrive at the entrance to the drive-in cinema I came to with Dada Zakiya, by the closed gate, far away from the city in a secluded area. The place is deserted and scary, not at all like the happy time I had here with Dada Zakiya. How alive the theatre was that evening; all one could hear was laughter and joyful conversation. Even the locals seated outside the theatre behind the walled space were having a great time watching a free show without the sound, making up their own dialogue and story. Dada Zakiya had told me that this theatre had magic, but I do not see any magic right now. I do not know why we are here. What have I got myself into? I control myself to avoid crying, but I feel a lump in my throat. No matter how many times I try to swallow, the lump remains, as if a marble is stuck there.

The *Muhindi* man removes a cigarette from a packet and leaves it unlit between his lips. He places the packet back on the dash and gets out of the car. He stands outside, leaning against the door as though he needs time to himself to think about what to do with us next. In the meantime, the policeman keeps an eye on us. Samuel sneakily tries to roll down the window with his elbow, which keeps slipping off the handle. Before long, another car arrives. Samuel and I look at each other. For the first time, I sense fear in Samuel, which terrifies me further. The *Muhindi* man approaches the other car and talks to the passenger in the back seat, who hands him a briefcase. They give each other a handshake and the car drives off.

The *Muhindi* man returns to the passenger seat and gives a thumbs-up to the policeman. "Okay, the deal is on." He takes a match and lights his cigarette.

The policeman blindfolds us before he drives out of

the theatre. I try to keep my senses alert and visualize the direction he is heading in. First he reverses, then turns right and drives straight ahead on a long road, further away from the city, probably to a small rural area. We drive for a long time on this endless road. I wonder if this road leads to the exclusive beach resorts that Dada Zakiya spoke of. But by now, I have lost all sense of direction and have no idea where we are. In fact, I have never been this far away from the city. Samuel screams for help. The *Muhindi* man shouts back at him and tells him to shut up, but Samuel takes his chances. The car stops and I hear a loud bang on Samuel. He stops shouting.

"Are you all right?" I whisper to Samuel. Samuel does not answer.

Please God, I pray. I hear Mama's words, "stealing is wrong." I continue to pray to God and make a promise that I will not steal again, *ever*. I think of Dada Zakiya. She would be extremely disappointed with me if she knew what I truly was.

The car turns onto bumpy pavement and slows down. After a short distance we reach a destination. "Get out!" the *Muhindi* man says and drags me out of the car. I hear a door open, and I am pushed inside and forced to a chair. He ties my hands behind the chair and removes the blindfold. The room is not very bright. I look around and do not see any sign of Samuel. "Who has been giving you the dollars for exchange?" the *Muhindi* man demands in his coarse voice.

"I don't know. My friend Samuel gets the money and I help him," I lie.

The policeman drags Samuel into the room, his face dripping with blood. He has hardly any strength left and collapses on the floor next to my chair. The policeman pours a bucket of water over him, and then they ask both of us for the name—threatening, screaming, shouting.

"Don't mention anything," Samuel manages to tell me, and he refuses to talk to them. They pick him up and drag him away to the other room. "Promise not to say a word to these bastards," Samuel shouts, collecting his strength as he is being taken away.

I hear louder screams from the other room, and then there is silence. Both the *Muhindi* man and the policeman come back, showing no remorse over what they have done to Samuel. I am more scared than ever, to the point that I hear myself panting and breathing heavily.

"Finish him if he doesn't speak," the *Muhindi* man says and leaves the room.

The policeman unties me from the chair, then ties both my hands back with a long rope and hangs me over a hook on the ceiling. He pulls down my shorts and underwear and throws them to the side. He takes a whip and slams it hard against my bare skin. Everything burns.

"Stop! Stop! Don't! Please stop!" I scream and cry.

"Give me those juicy balls!" He squeezes my testicles. "Let's pull them out for a souvenir."

I feel sick and vomit, and swallow part of it back down

my throat. "Keshavji brothers, Keshavji brothers," I barely manage to say.

"*Kuma mayo!* Those mother fuckers!" He drops the whip on the ground and leaves the room.

The hanging rope burns my hands, and my arms stretch in pain. I feel blood trickle down my bare buttocks and my testicles throb. I vomit again. Samuel opens the door and unties me. We run out and hide behind the bushes. After some time, we both realize that they have left us and are not coming back, and we are hiding from nobody.

"Why did you give them the name?" Samuel is fuming.

"Look at me." I raise my voice too. "I am naked. I am hurt." I hold my testicles tight to stop the pain and throbbing while I collapse on the ground.

Samuel gets down next to me and hits the ground with his fist. I notice that he is naked as well and bleeding a lot. He has been badly hurt. We go back inside and get our clothes. Then we walk through the bush until it gets dark and we cannot see our way. We settle by a tree and wait for daylight.

Samuel continues to shout. He blames me for giving the name. "You shit! You bloody sissy could not even take a little pain."

I have broken his dream of becoming rich, but I try to make him understand about the Keshavji brothers. "They don't give a damn about you. We got into this situation because of them. They must be dealing with dangerous people."

"You have ruined me. You idiot. You have destroyed me completely." Samuel believes that he was actually going to be safe and rich.

"Get over it. Go on, be a common thief. That's what you are good at," I say.

"Yes, you are right, brother, and you can be a loser, a stinky beggar," he retorts, insulting me.

I decide not to argue back. I have a better plan. I will do what Dada Zakiya teaches me to become. She is my true friend, my true sister. I will never let her down again.

sympathy
january 1981

THE NEXT MORNING, Samuel and I walk to the rural *shamba*, farm. We meet a group of women under the *banda* grinding dry corn in wooden mills. Children seated on mats are helping another group of women pack the flour.

"*Samhani*, sorry, Mama, please help us," Samuel says. "We were attacked by robbers yesterday. Look at what they did to us." He points to his bruised face.

The women stop their work, shake their heads and click their tongues. Some gasp, covering their mouths with their palms in disbelief. Samuel can be convincing, and charming too, if you do not know him. "While running away from the robbers, we may have turned in the wrong direction. We have lost our way to the city," Samuel adds.

"What are you boys going to the city for?" one of the women asks.

"To find jobs so we can look after our parents and younger siblings," Samuel says. "Please, if you could also offer us some water."

They let us use the tap next to the *banda*, which has a better flow than the city tap at the ferry berth. Samuel uses the water to drink and wash his wounds. He takes his sweet time while I eagerly wait my turn, fidgeting next to him. I remind myself to stay calm. I slip my hand into my shorts pocket and feel a bundle of dollars I had forgotten all about—left in my possession since yesterday's exchange. I quickly button up the flap and secure the pocket to prevent Samuel from finding out. I notice that his sling bag is not with him any longer. I try to remember if he had it with him in the car or if it dropped on the ground at the *sokoni* while we were being taken away. Either way, Samuel's money is gone. He shoulders me and walks back to the women. I quickly drink the water, which tastes muddy but quenches my thirst.

"A lorry will come by in the mid-afternoon to pick up the flour and deliver it to the city," one of the women offers. "I can ask the driver to give you a lift, if you boys wish. I am sure the driver will not mind." The rest of the women nod in agreement.

We sit beside the *banda* the entire morning, hungry, with no food or any offering from the farmers. In the early afternoon, the lorry arrives. The driver agrees to take

us to the city provided we help him unload at his destination. We take the offer, jump into the back of the lorry
and are on our way to the city.

Samuel and I decide to get our story straight in case
the Keshavji brothers find us. We agree to tell them that
we were robbed and know nothing about their names
being spoken.

"You cannot come back to my place and stay with me
any longer," Samuel says.

"No! Please, Samuel. I don't want to sleep on the
streets again. I will find work and still pay you," I plead.

He slaps me hard. "You!" He sticks his finger in my
forehead and pokes me. "If I see you anywhere near my
home, you are dead meat."

"I have my stuff, Mama's *kanga*, and my books with
all my earnings and expenses jotted. We need to calculate
my commissions. You have to pay me my money." I was
not going to let Samuel bully me and get away with it.

"You need what? Commission, huh!" He pushes me.
"Huh!" He pushes me again. "You shit, don't even think
about it."

I stand up over him. "I am coming to get my *kanga*," I
say firmly. He looks away. Then I remember the dollars
in my pocket and stay quiet, sitting at the other corner of
the lorry. Maybe I should not argue with him and should
get my *kanga* and books and leave. We do not talk all the
way.

Once we reach the city, we help the driver unload the

goods into the merchant's store. After that, we walk to the ferry berth.

Two *Wahindi* men stand guard by the ferry entrance. Samuel looks at me and I look at him. "Keshavjis' men," Samuel says. "You bloody fool. Now I can't even go home." He kicks my shin.

"Leave me alone, just leave me alone," I cry and run away.

I end up a stinky beggar once again, a loser back on the street. I cannot control my tears. I am tired. I am hungry. I am alone. More tears pour. I remind myself what Dada Zakiya told me: be patient. I nod to myself. What other choice do I have?

The night ladies notice me. "Why have you returned?" one of them asks.

"*Bahati mbaya*, bad luck," I say. I do not wish to talk anymore.

The ladies understand my pain and pat my back.

In the morning, I wait by the entrance of the Alliance Française for Dada Zakiya. I am not sure what time her class finishes. The wait seems longer than it might be, maybe because I crave her sympathy, to feel secure that I am not alone and am still capable of love and caring. My hands tremble every time I see a *Muhindi* man staring at me. I fear and worry that he might be one of the Keshavji brothers' people.

Dada Zakiya walks out of her college with her friend. "Juma, what happened to you?" She touches my bruised face.

"I was attacked by robbers last night. I guess it is the life of a street boy," I lie, but I make a promise to myself that this will be the last time.

"*Ema!* I am so sorry. Come with me to my home. I will ask Hamisi to rub some ointment on your bruises." She holds my hand. "*Ya khuda*, oh god, look at your shirt. It has a lot of bloodstains. You can have one of my clean t-shirts. Come, we can also have lunch together. *Haya*, ok?"

"Eew! Zakiya, you are disgusting. Don't touch him," her friend snaps.

"No, you are disgusting, so just get lost." Dada Zakiya dismisses her friend. Her friend gives me a nasty look and stomps away in anger.

I walk with my head down, fearing discovery, and pretend to scratch my forehead whenever someone comes close to us. The alley behind Dada Zakiya's flat smells of trash, as usual. We walk up the dirty stairs scattered with pigeon droppings. I notice chewing gum stuck to the wall, but there is none by the time we reach the third floor and the white gated door to the corridor leading to her flat.

Dada Zakiya rings the bell. "What is this?" Hamisi says. "You cannot bring him in."

"Keep quiet, Hamisi," she says, "and help me clean his

wounds. My friends did this to him. We will all go to jail if I don't help him. Let us clean him up and feed him. He has promised to shut up and not report me."

"I am not stupid, you know, Zakiya," he says as we enter.

Dada Zakiya looks down in embarrassment, and I am ashamed of myself.

Hamisi places some cotton wool and Dettol on the windowsill of the balcony for me to disinfect my wounds. I apply smelly Zam-Buk, which stings at first. Dada Zakiya allows me to use the bathroom to change into a clean t-shirt.

The flat is spotless. The floor shows streaks of water from the fresh mopping. On a wooden chest, incense sticks burn in a glass filled with uncooked rice. Next to the incense are various photographs of the family. Dada Zakiya invites me to sit next to her. I admire the glass ashtrays of different colours placed on each stool by the sofa set. The coffee table is stacked with albums, and there is a tape recorder next to it. Dada Zakiya inserts one of the cassettes and turns on *Muzungu* music that I have never heard before. "Put on some Hindi songs," I say.

"You are rejecting my Donny Osmond? I am going to marry him, you know," she says but changes the cassette anyway.

"*Haya tayari*, okay ready," Hamisi says. Dada Zakiya welcomes me to the dining chair to join her for lunch. The squeaky ceiling fan over the table keeps the flies away. Dada Zakiya washes her hands in the old white sink at the corner of the dining room. A green towel hangs over a thick nail and reads Bahari Resort. I wonder which of the two toothbrushes finely displayed in a flowery glass belongs to Dada Zakiya. Maybe the green one is hers, and the red must be Mama Fatima's. Dada Zakiya removes a cold jug of clear water from the fridge—I intend to drink all of it. I am in awe of the luxury of her lifestyle. Hamisi brings us *chhas*, a cold buttermilk drink with black pepper and cumin sprinkled over it, and serves us chicken curry with rice. Dada Zakiya motions to me to serve myself first.

I stack the rice on my plate, heaping it with three chicken legs and a huge potato. Dada Zakiya hands me a spoon. I laugh at her. "How can I fit the chicken into this spoon?" Dada Zakiya laughs too. I eat the food with my hands. The rice and curry are juicy and salty, and the cardamoms and cloves make it flavourful. We have it with yogurt and banana. Dada Zakiya eats a green chilly dipped in salt with every bite. I decide against that. Her welcoming home makes me forget my pain, and I silently pray that this lasts forever.

"Thank you, Dada, thank you so much," I say after our meal.

"*Shukrana*," she says. "Sharing brings *barakat*."

Hamisi frowns when he clears the table. Dada Zakiya ignores him and smiles at me. Still seated at the dining table, she picks up an album that has shells glued on the cover. It reminds me of the wonderful beach across the water by ferry, and saddens me. She shows me her father's pictures. "I miss him so much," she says. "I can't stop thinking of the accident. A lorry hit him on his way home from a safari. My father's car turned over six times, they say. I am glad he died immediately. It must have been painful." She stays silent for a while, staring at his photograph.

I turn the page. "Who is she?"

"*Dadima*, my grandmother."

Hamisi interrupts us. "You can go now," he tells me.

Dada Zakiya is mad at him. I agree with him. I should not put her to any trouble. "Thank you for your help," I tell Dada Zakiya. "*Ahsante*, Hamisi. Thank you for the delicious food," I tell him.

I walk out the clean corridor, through the shiny white gate, down the dirty stairs, exiting the smelly alley, back to the street to be a beggar—except this time I have three hundred dollars, and I do not know what to do with it.

Dada Zakiya comes by the salon the next day after her French class. "I have been worried about you. I had to come and see you," she says.

"I am fine now, Dada," I pretend. How can I tell her that I fear the Keshavji men? She gives me a packet of crisps and five shillings. "You are too kind." I hesitate before accepting her handout. She frowns, confused by my behaviour. "Dada, I have one more bad news to tell you."

"What, Juma?" she asks sympathetically.

"The robbers took my books away." I feel disgusted after the promise I made to myself never to lie to her again. Life has brought me to this situation, but I make the promise again.

"Don't worry. I will bring new books. You be safe now," she says, and leaves. Guilt, and her blind trust of me, tear me apart.

I remain standing on the footpath, refusing to beg. How can I go back to the rot? The thought crosses my mind to go to the *sokoni* and exchange the dollars I carry. I could rent the motel room for a few days and hide. Maybe by that time the Keshavji men will have given up searching for me. And if not, then at least I can have a few days of lavish lifestyle before they kill me. Maybe I can drink all the beer I refused when Samuel was offering it to me. Stupid me for trying to save money. What good did that do? My angry thoughts scare me, more than the fear of the Keshavji men finding me. No, no, I have to make things right or I will never forgive myself. I cannot trust anyone, especially myself, as long as I possess the money. Once again I ask for Mama's guidance. "Give me a sign, my angel. What shall I do?" Just then, my attention is drawn to a young girl sweeping the motel balcony. Her mother is a maid cleaning the rooms and training the girl to be a maid too. This gives me a thought.

I reach the steps of the Keshavji brothers' textile shop. Sweat trickles down my face and my throat feels dry. I close my eyes and ask my angel to stay with me so I can face whatever happens next. If I die today, killed, at least my conscience will be clear. My angel will be happy waiting for me.

I step into the shop. The younger Keshavji brother is attending a female customer, showing her different materials. His eyes widen when he sees me. He nods a couple of times and I wait. The customer cannot make up her mind. "Feel how soft the material is," he tells her. "It will make the best wrap for a maxi skirt." She continues to hold the fabric, stroking it as though it were her child. "Even Mama Zarina said this morning that this one was the best," he adds, knowing that if he mentions Mama Zarina, the best dressmaker in town, it will be a stronger sell. But the customer fusses and stares at the cloth. By now, the Keshavji brother is restless and wants to be rid of the customer. He does not really give a damn whether she buys or not, because for the Keshavji brothers, this textile shop is just a front. Their main business is done in the backroom. He finally asks the other worker to help the customer and signals me to follow him to the back.

The older, fat brother, seated in front of a fan wearing a *fulana*, undervest, and exposing his hairy body, is having tea and biscuits. "My, my, and look who decides to show up." He stands and lets out a fart, walks straight towards me and smacks my head. I quickly take the bundle of dollars and hand it to him. "What?" he says in surprise.

"Sir, has Samuel come to see you?" I ask in a shaky voice.

"No, but we had an expensive visit from two of his friends." He hits me again.

"Why are you hitting me? I am the one who has saved your money. Look at all the wounds and bruises I have taken for you." There is no doubt; I look like shit, so he has to believe me.

"Go on." He pulls the chair out and asks me to sit.

"You see, Samuel gave them your name, even though I asked him not to. I told him that you would come and rescue us, but he would not listen." I think I have got his attention. I speak furiously. "He did not pay me any commissions on the dollars we sold for you in the last few months either. He is a thief and will always be one."

The fat brother takes the money and has a discussion with the younger brother in private. They let me go with a warning that if I speak of them to anyone, I will not see another day. However, as long as I am safe with the brothers and have earned their trust, I might have got Samuel into bigger trouble. I could not give a damn about Samuel. He can face his own fate. As for me, I can put everything behind me and start fresh. "I promise to live an honest man," I tell my angel.

When I return to the street, the maid and the young girl are wrapping up their work, getting ready to go home. The girl notices me staring at her. I give her a smile. She comes towards me and asks if I want to tell her something.

"Yes! I want to thank you," I say.

"For what?" She is confused.

"For saving my life." I reach out to her and shake her hand.

"I don't even know you," she says but shakes my hand anyway.

"I had something that didn't belong to me," I tell her. "Watching you work today reminded me how important it is to make an honest living. Your mother must be *very* proud of you."

"So what did you do with the thing that didn't belong to you?" she asks.

"I returned it." I feel good confessing to a total stranger.

Her *matatu*, mini bus, arrives and she runs for it. She and her mother jump in. The *matatu* is full. Her mother manages to hang on tight to the door handle. The girl clings to her mother with one foot hanging out the door, yet she manages to look over her shoulder to give me a last glance.

idd
august 1981

IT IS FASCINATING to see so many Muslims fasting during the month of Ramadan. It reminds me that we humans are capable of tolerating hunger. The city is almost at a standstill during the lunch hour—workers lazing on the pavement, taxi drivers sleeping in their cars. Respectful Hindus and Christians eat discreetly at the half-empty restaurants. Despite the slow business, Jena Bai does not complain. Her workers say she fears God. "Once the Ramadan is over, she will turn into a witch again," one worker says. In the last several months, since my return to the street life, she is the only person who has never cared to ask where I was or if everything is okay with me. Her horrible words still ring in my ears: "You loser." But with the arrival of Josephine and her pimp on the street, Jena Bai is the least of my concerns.

On the other hand, Dada Zakiya continues to mentor me so that I can achieve my goal of a dignified life. At this point in my life, only her care and love keep me going. Even during Ramadan, while she fasts, she remembers to feed me, and even when her mouth is dry from thirst, she brings me a cold drink. "Go on, drink it. Don't feel guilty," she says.

I take a sip of cold water from a soda bottle. "I couldn't fast like you. You have a strong will," I say.

"I love the month of Ramadan," she says. "It is a total cleansing as a being. It is not about *not* eating. It is about life, appreciation, thanking God, understanding your purpose." She taps my hand softly. "You see, Juma, you may not know it, but you have a much stronger willpower. Don't think I am not aware that this food I've brought for you might be your only meal for the day." She stares at me as though wanting me to agree. I look away, knowing that if I acknowledged my willpower, I would be lying.

I change the tone of our conversation and tease her. "You don't need cleansing, you are already pure. Besides, if you fast one more day," I chuckle, "you'll be dead. Look at your face." I point at it and chuckle more.

"We are all born with survival instincts. I am sure that even if I had to live on the streets, beg, stay hungry and find a place at night to sleep, I could. In fact, I would. I am not the one who would die easily." She remains serious.

However, the truth is, she does not know the dangers and ugliness of the street life at night, things I have not told her. I am a daytime beggar to her. This is all she sees. I do not have the heart to tell her about Josephine's pimp, who recruits young, beautiful girls. He engages Josephine, who is younger than Dada Zakiya, with a few customers a night and keeps her money. Last week at almost midnight, when Josephine's customer left, the pimp forced her to go to the bar to offer her services again. He knew that the bar was about to close and there would always be one very drunk customer, desperate to pay her any price to sleep in the room for the rest of the night. But she hid in the back alley, crying. She was tired and wanted to sleep. He slapped her as usual when he caught her. Even though she has become my friend and I care for her, I walked away, pretending not to see or hear anything. This street turns you into a selfish human being at night.

"You are destined to live in a palace, not the streets. Don't even have those thoughts," I tell Dada Zakiya. "Imagine, once you become a doctor, you can live like a *maharani*, queen."

"No palace for me. It is not about money. I have a plan, a purpose," she says. "I will come back and open a dispensary in the village. This is my dream. Mother may not let me, but I will do it anyway." She smiles. "I will need you the most then. You are all I have. Will you come with me?

"Of course, if you're serious," I say. "It is not easy. A

village life, I mean. There is no electricity, no fridge or ceiling fan. Think about it."

"I will have you as my strength. But you must make me a promise." She focuses on a plan and seriously talks of the future. I listen to her attentively, no time to chuckle or joke anymore. She writes a ten-year plan in my exercise book and the accomplishments she expects. I make her a promise that for the next ten years before she returns, I will read every day and never give up learning. In the meantime, I will get out of the street life and make a decent living.

The loudspeaker at the mosque comes on. The *Azan*, Muslim call to prayer, starts. The city is reminded that it is soon after sunset. There will be breaking of the fast after the prayers. "*Ya khuda!* I'm in trouble. It's already past six. Where did the time go?" Dada Zakiya says. "Mother is going to be very cross with me. I better run." She rushes back home.

I take full advantage of the Ramadan and visit Jena Bai for *futuru*, food offering, to break the fast. She knows I do not fast, but I think she also knows that I could knock at the door of any Muslim home during Ramadan and be given a share of food, even though I am a total stranger. Dada Zakiya told me that her mother keeps loaves of bread handy to give out to anyone who knocks at her door. Jena Bai nods and gives me a small bowl of boiled rice with a spoonful of tomato sauce poured over it, but still she does not smile.

I look forward to the Idd festivals in the next two days, at the end of Ramadan. Dada Zakiya has promised to share the offering she receives for Idd. After Idd *Namaz*, prayers, in the morning, family and friends will exchange *mithhai*, Indian sweets. Dada Zakiya tells me that she gets lots of money from her uncles and aunts. She does not fancy *mithhai* but looks forward to the Cadbury Whole Nut chocolate from London that her aunt sends her every Idd. "I love chocolates. It's a once-a-year treat, so scrumptious."

The butcher on the street is busy with orders. A fully loaded pickup arrives with whole halal goats. The workers' long white jackets are smudged with blood as they put one goat at a time over their shoulder and take it to the butchery. Mama Fatima rushes out of the salon and makes her order.

"Hamisi will be preparing goat biryani for the family and himself the day before," Dada Zakiya says, revealing the feast menu. She asks me to meet her by the Darkhana gates on Idd at twelve noon when she comes for a community lunch and *dandhiya-raas*, festive dances and music.

"*Idd Mubarak*, Happy Idd, Juma," Dada Zakiya says, wearing a beautiful white dress and a stylish silver clip on the right side of her perfect shoulder-length hair. "For you." She hands me two full bags. "I have lots of assorted *mithhai*, goat biryani and soda." She smiles and tucks twenty shillings in my pocket. "I got a total of one hundred shillings cash in gifts. I will spend the remaining eighty on Hindi cassettes," she whispers secretively. I accept the auspicious meal and think of Josephine. I will share the spirit and celebrate with her tonight when her pimp is not watching.

Dada Zakiya twists her left wrist, showing me her watch. "It's my grandmother's. Mother tells me that at nineteen, I am responsible and old enough to own it."

Her friend comes by and they hug each other. "*Idd Mubarak.*" Holding their *dandhiya*, dancing sticks, painted in red and green, they walk into the gates of Darkhana and join the happy crowd. I hear live drums playing and dance to the end of the street till the sound fades off.

Dada Zakiya proudly tells me the history behind the remarkable watch that once belonged to her grandmother. "It's a boy, it's a boy." Dada Zakiya's grandfather celebrated when her father was born and delivered *mithhai* to families and friends. He presented grandmother with a watch as if she were a queen, and it became the talk of the town. Women envied grandmother. Many of them made excuses to come and see the baby, but they paid more attention to the watch.

Dada Zakiya lets me hold the watch. I inspect every part of it. A fancy upside down U is engraved at the back of the dial, and underneath it reads OMEGA. Tiny print at the bottom reads SWISS MADE. I am amazed that the dial not only shows the time but also has a hand for timing seconds. "You wind this button so it keeps on ticking and ticking and ticking," Dada Zakiya explains. "And if you click this, look, then you can time the seconds." We experiment by holding our breath, and I hold mine twice as long as she does. She gives up and calls me the winner. I tease her, "and you have never even smoked."

"Don't remind me of that disgusting habit of yours. I am still mad at you."

"Sorry, Dada, I have sworn to never do it again. I will not, *haki ya Mungu*, promise upon God's name." I actually mean it; besides, I cannot afford it anyway. I used to steal one or two cigarettes from Samuel's packet when he fell asleep. He never suspected or smelled it on my breath, but Dada Zakiya? No one can fool her.

"You've been smoking?" she said, sniffing my mouth.

"No, Dada." I made it worse by lying.

She pressed her lips tightly together and stood tall with her hands on her hips. That day I had to learn all about lungs and cancer, a never-ending lecture. For my weekly homework, I had to write I WILL NOT SMOKE AGAIN one hundred times daily. That was a difficult task, as I was busy with the black market business during the daytime, so I would stay up late at night.

"What's your problem, brother? Why the bloody hell are you studying?" Samuel's pressure made it tougher.

The worst was quitting smoking. Samuel tried to convince me not to study anymore and forget about Dada Zakiya. He did not understand that she is the one person I will never forget.

I smile at Dada Zakiya. "Tell me more about grandmother," I say.

She puts the watch back on her wrist and gives it a kiss. "Grandmother was a star in the household for giving birth to a boy. She was twenty-one." Dada Zakiya tells it as though she were there herself. "Grandmother used to spend hours at night combing my hair and massaging my head with coconut oil as she told me about her life, as I now tell you, Juma." She smiles. "Imagine, this watch has been ticking for over fifty years."

"Wow!" I am amazed.

"I will make it tick for another fifty. What do you say, Juma?"

"Brilliant!" I say. We spend hours admiring the watch, and Dada Zakiya talks endlessly about her grandmother.

toast
december 1981

DADA ZAKIYA IS flying in the clouds, blissfully happy. She holds a file close to her heart, as though it is her baby, containing the papers she needs for a medical checkup and x-rays for the immigration visa. "This is it, Juma!" she says. "You know what this means? I can't believe the time has come." We walk for a good half hour, and all she speaks of is her dreams and the life she imagines having on the other side of the ocean.

We reach Agakhan hospital and enter through the magnificent front garden. The breeze and roaring waves of the ocean add joy to its beauty. Even the bungalows adjacent to the hospital give a classy touch to the area. "Wait for me here in the shade." She points at a mango tree by the entrance. "I will get the examinations done quickly."

I take a moment and plan how to pluck the irresistible seasonal fruits hanging above me out of reach. I pick up a stone, close one eye and target a mango that looks deliciously ripe. I know I can aim perfectly. I swing my hand, but just then a nurse passes by pushing an old man in a wheelchair. "Aah! A pleasant afternoon browse," the old man says. The nurse pays no attention to him. Her eyes are set on me and she almost tips the wheelchair over the edge of the pavement. She continues with her nasty stare until I drop the stone and walk away from the tree. I browse through the garden, moving to the other side away from the nurse's view, and instead pluck flowers from the jasmine bush for Dada Zakiya before settling on the path next to the entrance.

"All done." Dada Zakiya comes back and checks her watch. "That was almost two hours. Sorry, I didn't realize it would take so long."

"I didn't mind." I give her the flowers. "For luck."

She smells the flowers, puts them in her pocket and gives me a soft pat on my sweaty head. Then she brushes her palm over her jeans and wrinkles her nose. "Why did you not sit under the tree, *gandho*, silly?" She laughs.

I give one more look at the mangoes and then at the nurse, who still pays no attention to her patient but seems relieved to see me go. There is always tomorrow, I think, and I know where the mangoes are.

Dada Zakiya takes me to the *panwallah's* shop for a celebration. She orders two cold glasses of freshly made passion fruit juice and a plate of samosas. She teaches me how to toast. We raise our glasses and give them a soft clink. She explains, "This is when you say, 'For Dada, good wishes for your new life and new adventures,'" and I repeat the words. Then she raises her glass higher and says, "and to you, my best friend, good wishes for your new life and new adventures."

"My life? *Wapi* Dada, that remains the same."

"Actually, I have a surprise for you." She raises her brows.

"Huh!"

"My friend's brother knows a manager at the hotel by the beach. They are renovating a snack bar in the swimming pool area. Once it's completed, he plans to hire servers." She smiles. "He has agreed to interview you. It's just a matter of time. Now we both wait."

"Dada Zakiya, my gosh! Are you . . . sure?" I fall out of my chair.

"I keep my promises. Always remember that." She reaches out to help me up as if I was as light as a feather.

"I never doubted you." I touch her hand and get up, and sit back on the chair.

"Well, that calls for a double celebration," she says. We clink our glasses one more time and sip the tangy juice.

Before paying the bill, she places an order. "One *mittho paan* please, uncle, without *sopari*, betel nut, and also pack four samosas."

Uncle prepares the sweet *paan*, pasting rose syrup on the betel leaf, then sprinkling fennel seeds, coriander seeds, sweetened grated coconut and something else sweet. Dada Zaikya doesn't know what it is, and uncle is not interested in telling us. He folds the *paan* in a triangle shape like samosas and wraps it in paper.

"Never mind the ingredients. Just try it and you will want more." Dada Zakiya laughs and then bites half the *paan* and puts the other half in my mouth. My mouth is so full that I can barely speak to thank her. Juicy *paan* refreshing my mouth. She smiles at me and hands me the pack of samosas to go.

For the next three months, Dada Zakiya and I spend a lot of time talking of our plans. She waits in anticipation for her medical reports to clear, but it may take a while. She has heard that sometimes it takes as long as six months.

"I am in no hurry for your departure. I cannot imagine my life without your guidance and care. Don't forget me," I say sadly.

"You will be present in my thoughts every day. I will especially think of you the day I have a stethoscope around my neck," she says.

"And I will wait for your return. On that day, I will touch and feel that stethoscope in my hands."

We gaze at each other, lost in our own dreams.

~

I go to the entertainment side of the beach and settle under the tree where Mama used to sit on Sundays and beg. "Go on, be free for a while. Do whatever you want to, son," she would say. "I will make enough without you from these generous and joyful people." Since then, many Sundays have come and gone, but the real freedom is yet to come. As Dada Zakiya says, it is just a matter of time.

Before long, the beach crowd multiplies. People dance and sing the songs from today's movie—I bet—and gather around the busy vendors. Boys get sillier than silly, sticking their tongues out at the girls or making farting sounds with their mouths. The girls giggle, with the exception of an odd one or two grouchy ones who push the boys or scream to get them into trouble. A group of young children run towards the shore, and their grandparents panic. "Don't touch the water, you will drown!" they shout and run to grab them.

I walk towards one mother, who struggles to quieten her baby's screeching cry. I click my tongue to a tune, and the baby pays attention to my sound and giggles. The relieved mother rocks the baby and sings till the baby falls asleep. "*Ahsante*, that was very nice of you," she says and calls her husband. "Give him some baksheesh." The husband hands me five shillings, my first earning—not by begging or stealing—and it feels good.

I whistle and queue at the *chana bateta* vendor. The previous customer returns the tin bowl and drops it in a bucket of water. The vendor shakes the bowl out of the bucket, scoops a serving for me and pours coconut chutney over it. I reach into the bucket of water to find a clean spoon. A truly blessed meal I have earned today, I think to myself, and sit under the tree to eat. I hope you see this, Mama. I will make you very proud of me, just wait and see. Then an unexpected thing happens when I return the bowl. Someone grabs me from behind and pulls my t-shirt around my neck. I turn to defend myself, but the punch to my face throws me to the ground sideways and I hurt my elbow. I quickly stand up and scream. In front of me is Samuel, and I freeze. No way, Samuel is back. He comes closer to me and pokes me hard in the chest.

"Hey! Not here. Take your business elsewhere. We work here." The vendor is not impressed at all.

Ignoring the vendor, Samuel and I continue with our unfinished business. "I was thrown into a pickup by the Keshavji brothers' men. Do you know where they took me? Huh! Do you? You shit." He pushes me. "They took me far into a jungle and left me to bleed to death. I didn't know where I was. My hand was broken, and look at my nose. I can't even breathe properly," and he pushes me further. "I crossed the Savannah, almost got eaten by the lions, was hospitalized for months in that disgusting ward, but I lived with one hope—to come back and ruin you."

"Listen!" I block him. "We are even. You kept all my commissions and Mama's *kanga*, too. I told you to leave me alone." I am furious. "Now get lost! I don't give a shit what happened to you. I've been living on the streets since that day, you selfish bastard."

The vendor grabs Samuel. "You leave. Now!" Samuel takes a step back and spits in my face. I pick up a stone and he runs away, and I notice a slight limp in his left leg. With that scarred face and disfigured nose, he looks like the monster he is. I worry. I know this is not the last I will see of him. It has been such a relief without him for over a year. But this time I will not let him interfere in my life. Not again.

"Juma!" Dada Zakiya says, thrilled to see me.

"Dada Zakiya, what are you doing here?"

"You know, Sunday outing, with mother and friends." She looks at my hand. "Are you okay?"

"Yes, Dada."

She frowns. "Zakiya! Zakiya!" Mama Fatima calls her from a distance.

"I've got to go," she says, and she runs back to her mother.

They both look at me and it seems they are arguing, as always. But I am glad she left before noticing my scraped elbow, or else there would have been a thousand questions followed by a thousand lies.

Dada Zakiya and her friend jump on the hood of the car and chat as they eat. I stand by the tree and watch them. When I glance around, Samuel is still there, watching me with a look that makes me very uncomfortable. He points at me, threatening. Then he turns towards

Dada Zakiya and points at her. I do not know what he means to tell me, but my gut says he does not have good intentions.

interview
march 1982

"YOU ARE A perfect Englishman," Dada Zakiya says. "Don't you look handsome?" She flatters me while I stand proudly in front of her, dressed in a crisp white cotton shirt, black trousers and English-style shoes—all from her cousin. For some reason the clothes did not suit his taste any longer.

"I am really nervous." I stretch my hands out to show Dada Zakiya how they tremble.

"Take a deep breath. Your lungs need some oxygen," she advises.

I close my eyes and breathe deeply enough to fill my lungs. I hiss as I breathe out, and amazingly the trembling stops.

"Better?" She massages my shoulders. "Now, let's rehearse once more." She checks the time. "You have one more hour. Now remember, your first impression is very important."

"I know. I will walk tall and straight."

"With confidence," she reminds me.

I cannot believe that in an hour I have an interview with the poolside manager at the hotel, arranged by Dada Zakiya's friend's brother. Dada Zakiya has worked hard to prepare me for the interview, teaching me how to walk and talk. She has also taught me some new, sophisticated English sentences, such as *It is a pleasure to meet you* when I shake the manager's hand.

"I will pretend to be the manager, so let's get started." She sits by the stairs behind Mama Fatima's salon.

I stand straight with confidence and walk towards her. Just then, Dada Zakiya screams loud enough for the entire city to hear. It happens so fast—Samuel always has an escape plan—and grandmother's Omega watch is gone.

"Samuel! No!" I scream louder than Dada Zakiya as I run to chase him, but it is too late. I return to Dada Zakiya to make sure she is fine.

Mama Fatima, Maria and their customers rush out to tend to Dada Zakiya's frightened scream. "Dadima's watch! No! No!" Dada Zakiya shakes and wails. "That *chor*, thief, snatched it from my wrist." Mama Fatima strokes her hair and grabs her close, just like the mother at the beach who rocked her baby. "He came so fast and grabbed my wrist, Mother," Dada Zakiya cries.

"*Bas . . . bas . . . bas . . .* It's okay, *beta*, child," Mama Fatima says to soothe her.

I stand helpless, my heart breaking. "Dada, don't cry. I will get it back for you."

"And you, Juma, I heard you call his name. Do you know him? How could you!" Dada Zakiya shouts.

"I told you before, Zakiya," Mama Fatima says angrily and stops stroking her hair. "You can't trust these people, but you just don't listen." She looks directly at me. "Get lost from here right away. Go before I call the police and have you put in jail. *Ondoka!*"

I do not budge. "Dada, I did not know. Like I said, I will get it back for you, I promise." I try to make eye contact with her but she looks away.

"Zakiya, no more. This is it." Mama Fatima continues to scold her. "Enough roaming around the town. I have given you too much freedom. Just because you don't have a father does not mean you can do whatever you want while I work hard bringing you up." The customers try to calm her, but by now she is shakier than Dada Zakiya, which does not help the situation. A faint murmur arises from the people gathered in the parking lot, most probably making up their own stories.

In the meantime, Dada Zakiya pays no attention to her surroundings. "I trusted you, Juma, I trusted you." She keeps uttering these words to me. My heart shatters into a million pieces.

"Maria, tell this boy to disappear before . . ." Mama

Fatima does not bother to finish the sentence. She grabs Dada Zakiya's hand and pulls her inside the salon.

"You heard her," Maria tells me firmly, "or would you like me to translate the meaning of disappear."

"I didn't know, Maria, trust me. I will get her watch back."

"Lies, you are full of lies," Maria says. "You know the thief. One doesn't show up at the back of the salon to steal the watch unless it's planned. You are a liar, you have shamed me."

"I will prove it to you," I say. "Tell Dada Zakiya to trust me."

I rush out and walk the town, searching for Samuel at every possible spot he might be found. In the late afternoon, despite my dry mouth from the sharp sun, I frantically repeat my search to be absolutely sure I have not missed him. I feel a huge lump in my throat when Samuel does not show up at the ferry berth to go home. He wanted revenge and he got it; he ruined me as planned. His quest is over and he is gone.

At dusk, I return to the street, exhausted, and collapse at the back of the salon. I must not give up. Think, Juma, think, I say to myself. Could he be at Halima's? Every time we missed our ferry, Samuel would take me to Halima's place. Halima worked for various families as an *aya*, nanny. She would never last at her job—by choice. She was a thief and would pretend to work as an *aya*, and once she had earned the homeowners' trust, they would give her the freedom to be home alone with their children. She would steal things from the house and never return.

Halima was Samuel's girlfriend, sort of, but only when it was convenient for him. She lives in the slums behind the cheap movie theatre, in the dirtiest part of town where they show all the Bruce Lee movies. Day or night, the area is disgustingly stinky where the slum children dig deep holes, huge enough to fit a Volkswagen Beetle, to dispose of city trash. Once the hole is full, they set the trash on fire and then cover it up with sand the next day. In the meantime, another hole is dug for another dump, but the smell lingers. Younger children stand by the stink all day, waiting for a driver from the rich area to arrive so they can help him dispose of the trash for a minimal fee. I remember one incident when a very young girl poured kerosene and lit the trash on fire while she stood in the middle of the pit. Screams and shouts were heard, but no one could save the girl. Her charred body was impossible to retrieve, and it turned into ashes together with the trash. Every time I think of her, I realize how unpredictable life is, and the incident with Samuel today has proven it.

I reach Halima's place, made of corrugated tin. I have no time to be polite. I barge in. Samuel, the shameless bastard, is receiving a free job from Halima on the dirty ground. I grab him and kick him in his privates, wishing they would become unusable. Halima screams and runs to the corner. "Give me the watch, give it to me," I demand. He punches my face. I punch back and knock his head. Samuel grabs me and we roll on the ground. Halima jumps in between us to break up the fight. "Samuel, give me the watch back, I mean it," I say.

"Or what?" he asks.

"I will kill you. Trust me, I will."

Samuel laughs mockingly and puts on his trousers. He pulls the watch out of his pocket. "All right, here you go, brother," he says. When I reach to grab it, he punches my stomach. I gag and drop to the ground. "If you can get it out of my pocket, then the watch is yours. I will never sell it, this is my promise. You see, brother, I am the best *mwizi* and you will never be able to catch up with me." He drags me out of the shack and throws me on the dirt. "Don't mess with me again, brother. Today I just took her watch. Next time, I will not be gentle."

I get up and run. I run as fast as I can. I fall on the path on a dark street. I cannot go any further. I feel useless. I do not know what to do. My dreams are shattered. Mama told me that *maskinis* are not allowed to dream. I probably should not have. Maybe God is punishing me for my sins for lying to Dada Zakiya and for choosing the wrong path, and I deserve to be on the streets.

It may be too late to ask for Dada Zakiya's forgiveness, but I must tell her about Samuel. I do not trust him. She must be careful.

freedom kiosk
march 1982

DADA ZAKIYA SCREAMS, "Juma, help me! Help me!"

I am tied to the tree and struggle to free myself. The rope tangles around my neck. The moment I move, I die. Dada Zakiya cannot see me but I see her clearly.

"Help me, Juma!" she screams. "Juma, where are you?"

I twist my wrists to untie the knot so I can remove the rope around my neck and rest of the body. Realizing how tight the knot is, I panic. My breathing races and sweat rushes down my forehead. I feel a soft touch on my hand and hear Mama whisper, "I am here, I will free you." I run to rescue Dada Zakiya.

Samuel holds her tight against his chest, a knife at her neck. She turns red and has no more strength to scream. "Let her go!" I shout. Samuel looks at me, slurps his lips and slits her throat. "No, Dada!" I wake up with a scream on this dark street, panting and sweating. I stay up for the rest of the night. I fear, I fear.

In the early morning, I rush to Dada Zakiya's flat. A rusty brass padlock dangles from the gated door, and I see that the entrance to the front door is locked. Where could she be this early on Sunday when she prefers to sleep, unless she has been locked in? I ring the bell, but no one answers. Something is not right. Everything feels off balance.

I wait downstairs in vain. At almost four in the afternoon, I leave. Even though the town is silent because of the two o'clock Sunday driving curfew, my mind is cluttered with noise, and none of it makes sense. I walk in the middle of the road with my eyes closed to clear my thoughts. My heart pounds in fear, but I continue to walk blindly till I feel as light as a feather. I should have told Dada Zakiya about Samuel a long time ago, but now is no time for regrets; it is time to plan how to get the watch back.

I open my eyes and find myself at the petrol station. Two suspicious young boys fiddling with the pump startle when they see me. One of them stands defiantly. "Go find your own pump to sniff petrol if you are hungry," he says. I raise my hand in surrender, but an *askari* comes from behind and chases us out of the station. The boys run to the corner of the shop and pull out a bottle of glue from their pocket. I am scared I will become one of them. "Forgive me, Dada, forgive me," I scream like a madman, and frighten the boys away.

Later that night, I find my pen on the doorstep behind Mama Fatima's salon, at the spot where laughter turned into tears. A metre away, I pick up my exercise book, messed up with a muddy shoeprint as though it had been stepped on on purpose. I browse through the pages to see if the ten-year plan is still there. The words and the drawings smile at me, telling me not to give up, but I do not know what to do.

I need Josephine tonight. She is standing against the pole by the restaurant. I long to speak to her, but her pimp stands guard next to her. A customer arrives and the pimp negotiates with him. Then Josephine and the customer get into a taxi and leave. I wait for her to come back. Jena Bai leaves, the bar closes, the street lights dim, even the mice disappear, but Josephine never returns to the motel. I feel lonelier than I have ever felt. I jot in my book:

DADA ZAKIYA HAS TO TRUST ME
DADA ZAKIYA HAS TO TRUST ME
DADA ZAKIYA HAS TO TRUST ME
DADA ZAKI. . .

In the morning, I stay away from Maria and sneak out of the street to avoid any confrontation with her. I sit on the bench at the clock-tower park and stare at the pages in my book for the longest time. Not enough lines. Dada

Zakiya would expect more. I must write more. Hunger taunts me, makes me cry. I remember the twenty shillings in my pocket that Dada Zakiya gave me yesterday for good luck.

I order *mandazi* and chai at Kanji Bhai's teashop. "Do you have money?" Kanji Bhai asks bluntly. I do not blame him. He has seen me beg for food, which he lately has not been handing out.

"Yes, *bwana*." I give him twenty shillings.

He inspects it. "Did you steal it?"

"I got it as a gift."

"And who the hell is going to give you a gift *heh*? *Chor salo*, damn thief." He hands me the change back and gives me my food.

I gather my courage to face Dada Zakiya once more and visit her home. "You have a bloody nerve," Hamisi says. His head trembles in anger as though he is about to push me down the stairs and kill me.

"Please, I must see her, I must." I shake the gate, begging to come in.

"She is gone, it is too late now." His voice drops.

"Gone . . . what do you mean gone?"

"Mama Fatima sent her away to her auntie's for a month. She cried too much and did not want to live here anymore. She hates you and hates this country. She wants to go away and never come back." He goes back inside, slamming the door.

This cannot be happening. Oh Mama, please tell me

this is a bad dream and wake me up. Mama does not respond.

Word spreads on the street. Maria probably told one of the night ladies about the watch incident while grooming her hair. I am classified as a thief, a boy who will stab you in the back. Everyone has turned against me and asked me to move out of the street. I am prohibited from visiting my home—my garage—and Josephine at night. Where do I go? What am I to do?

Day after day, I roam around Dada Zakiya's house and hide under the stairs. I pass by her French class, but she is nowhere to be seen. Could she still be at her auntie's? It's over a month. Why is she not returning? Dada, please come back.

Four months pass and I am once again at Dada Zakiya's flat, hoping Hamisi will not ignore the doorbell this time. At some point, he will have to open the door and talk to me. A *Muhindi* lady comes out and stands behind the gated door. I give her my best smile. I am so happy to see her; she must be Dada Zakiya's auntie. Dada Zakiya is back! I am very sure she is eagerly waiting to see me.

"*Nani?* Who is it?"

"*Jambo*, Mama. Is Dada Zakiya home?" I rise on tiptoe and look over her shoulder, certain that I will see Dada Zakiya standing right behind her.

"Zakiya?" She frowns.

"Yes, Dada Zakiya, my Dada," I say.

"Ah, you mean Fatima? Sorry, I am the new owner. She and her family have left the country. This is my home now," and she attempts to go back into her flat.

"Mama, Mama," I call her in panic. She waits for me to talk.

"Left the country? When? Is Hamisi here?" I say, sweating and shaking. What am I hearing?

"No, son. We did offer him the job but he refused. He said he was old and needed to return to his village and retire. Fatima settled him well. *Samhani*, sorry, I cannot help you." She disappears inside.

In a flash my life turns into hopelessness. I can barely walk. My legs tremble and I lose my sense of balance, missing a step and tumbling down the last few stairs. Pain in my body, pain in my heart, pain everywhere. "No!" I look up and cry, "No God no, don't do this to me, I beg of you, I beg of you." People pass me as if I am invisible, up the stairs, down the stairs, no one cares, no one cares.

A *Muzungu* lady wearing a *kitenge* dress, African kimono, stands with her hands on her hips outside Mama Fatima's salon, watching the sign writer lift a new board over the entrance of the salon. I stand next to her, curiously. She smiles at me and looks back at the sign going up.

"Maria!" I am so happy to see her. "Maria, please, you

have to tell me where Dada Zakiya is."

Maria cries. This strong-hearted woman has a soft side after all, a side I have never seen. "Fatima and Zakiya have left the country. They are gone. And we have to deal with it."

"Why? Why?" I cry with her. She hugs me. "I did not plan with Samuel to steal the watch," I say. We continue to hug.

"I know. Josephine told me." She lets me go. "She came to see me last month to have her hair braided and told me all about Samuel and you. You did make some bad choices with him and got yourself into this situation, Juma. But I know, now, that you never meant to harm Zakiya."

"Does she know? Did you tell her? Please say yes. Please tell me Dada Zakiya knows and she trusts me."

"Zakiya never came back from her auntie's. It happened so fast. Fatima went to her sister's to pick up Zakiya and they left the country from there. I did tell Fatima. She knows." Maria pats my head. I wipe her tears. "Let's believe that Zakiya knows." She smiles. "By the way, you are welcome on this street."

We stay silent, lost for words. Mama Fatima will never tell Dada Zakiya of my innocence. Mama Fatima will not want Dada Zakiya to come back. But Dada Zakiya will have to speak to her heart and trust herself.

The *Muzungu* lady claps. Maria and I look up at the sign.

Freedom Kiosk
Bead Braids and Fresh Coffee Shop

"Do you like it?" the *Muzungu* lady asks Maria.

"Very much so, Mrs. Scott."

Maria introduces me to Mrs. Scott. "This is Juma. You were searching for a coffee server and kiosk helper. This is your boy. He speaks perfect English. He is educated and trustworthy."

"Well, hello, Juma. It is nice to meet you." Mrs. Scott gives me a soft handshake.

I glance at Maria in surprise. She gives me a nod with a smile.

"My pleasure, Mrs. Scott." I give her a firm handshake just as Dada Zakiya had taught me. With confidence, Juma, with confidence, she would say.

Mrs. Scott gives me a look of approval. "Come back tomorrow. We shall talk then."

I look up at the sign. *Freedom Kiosk.* Indeed, I think to myself.

two

josephine

I WAS IN love with Josephine the first time I saw her. My heart skipped a beat and then it beat faster than normal. I gave it a thump with my fist and sat on the path admiring this seventeen-year-old beauty. I clearly remember her wearing a white dress with a thick leather belt tightly wrapped around her waist—shiny black—which made her hips look fuller. Her incredibly smooth skin did not need any makeup; her stunning beauty shone through without it. Everything about her was perfect—except for the sadness in her smile. She stood at the corner all by herself, away from the other night ladies. I was not sure why no one talked to her, so I introduced myself to make her feel more welcome on the street.

Her pimp showed up unexpectedly and stood right in front of my face. "She is very expensive, you shitty little bastard," he said. His coarse voice and big, red, drunken eyes scared me so much that I stepped back at once. Josephine ran to the other side of the pole, almost tripping even though the path was clear. She stuck her fingers in her mouth, biting her nails, and swayed her upper body forward and backward. I realized right away that I had got her into trouble. The pimp pointed his finger at me. "You want to have some fun there, boy? There are plenty of men interested in young boys too." He stomped heavily towards Josephine and slapped her. What surprised me was that Josephine had no expression on her face—she showed no emotion at all. One slap, two slaps, she stood there, accustomed to it all.

Every time I witnessed those slaps, I thought of the man who tortured me and was prepared to pull out my testicles. Would I have become accustomed to the pain and beating if I had let him? If so, then maybe I would not have needed to give them the Keshavjis' name. But there I was, at fifteen, back on the streets, a pathetic beggar. I was weak, a boy without courage, who could not even stand up for Josephine. Or was I selfish? The last thing I needed was another problem added to my life— the pimp.

Knowing what he was capable of doing to me, I kept my distance and stayed in a lit area. He was ruthless and carried a knife, which I am sure he would not have hesitated to use. Josephine ignored me when he was around. Once in a while, she would sneakily glance at me. She knew I was watching her all the time, but not even once she exchanged a smile.

One night the pimp passed out on the street drunk, his big, muscular body lifeless. The night ladies and their customers dragged him to the back of the parking lot and dumped him by the trash. I was tempted to break a bottle of beer on his head. No one would have known. Then again, I had sinned enough, I had wronged enough. God had given me a second chance; there would not be a third, so I left the scene. Was I wrong to make such a decision? I regretted it at times, especially whenever I saw Josephine suffer. But then it also made me work harder to get out of the street life, which was the only way to save Josephine too.

Later that night, I knocked on Josephine's door once her customer had left. I told her about the pimp getting dumped by the trash. She burst into hysterical laughter. What a change in her mood; I was not expecting such a reaction. I thought she might run to tend to him, out of fear or because she really did care for him, but instead she kept laughing. She was happy, happy to know that he had suffered. Then she let me in the room. That was the night Josephine and I became secret friends.

We spoke of Dada Zakiya. Josephine loved her, even though they had never met. "She is a goddess," Josephine would say.

I told her about Samuel, how selfish he had always been and how I got myself into bad situations with him.

"You are lucky," she said. "At least he is gone. Look at me. I am still stuck with the devil."

Josephine's mother was a *malaya*, a cheap hooker. She worked in front of the Pombe House. When Josephine was twelve, her mother became very sick. Her medical expenses were so high she knew she would not be able to support her daughter, so she sold Josephine to a pimp who was looking for a young virgin. Josephine's pimp was paid a lot of money for her first services.

"My mother barely got ten percent, or maybe less, out of what the pimp made on my first job." Josephine spat on the ground, disgusted. "There were three of them. Three!" She paused, trying to catch her breath.

"It's okay, you don't need to tell me." In truth, I did not want to hear it.

She ignored me and continued to talk. "Two of them stood naked waiting their turn, laughing and drinking beer, while the first one lay atop, hurting me. I did not scream or shout. I uttered no sound."

"Let it go, Josephine," I said.

She stared at the ground. "My mother gave me some advice when she said her goodbyes. She told me to accept whatever came along and not to ever cry, and practise not to feel pain." Her voice was shaky. "I accepted, I did not cry, but the pain remains, and I still feel it."

"Sh! Sh!" I hugged her.

She pushed me away, frustrated, grinding her teeth, and dropped to the ground wailing. I sat down next to her and held her hand. I could feel her tremble, I could feel her pain. I moved closer to her, wrapping my arms around her in a tight hug.

"And what do I get?" she said. "A place to live with that devil pimp, and to fulfil his exotic desires too. I am tired, Juma, I am tired."

I continued to hold her tight. She finally relaxed and let go.

a day at work
july 1984

THE GLASS CHIMES over the window in the Freedom
Kiosk reflect onto Mrs. Scott's face. She puts on her
sunglasses and takes a seat by the counter. With her head
down, she writes. I am not sure what she writes, but she
does every morning. I once glanced at her diary and saw
the words *the day I met Danny.* Don't we all have such
stories about the day we met that special person? I hope
her meeting with Danny ended with a happy story, not a
sad and hurtful one like mine.

I turn on the coffee brewer and place the cups and sau-
cers next to it. The aroma energizes the room. I put the
flask of fresh milk and bowl of sugar to one side. Maria's
first three customers arrive at their usual time and the
morning goes by smoothly. By the afternoon, the kiosk
fills with tourists. My job is to serve the customers special

complimentary local coffee that Mrs. Scott has perfected, the best brew in town. On their way out, most of the tourists buy tins of coffee as a gift to take home.

This may not be the dream job I had anticipated—a waiter at a classy beach resort—but at this point in my life, I am fine where I am. And it's amazing how much I have improved my English skills in the last two years, which is one of the advantages of working for a *Muzungu*. The bigger advantage of working at Mrs. Scott's kiosk is that it keeps me closer to Josephine. Even more, it has got me out of the street and given me new hope. Today, now that I'm eighteen, street life would have been much tougher. I was losing my childish charm, and sympathy for me was fading. If it had not been for Maria, I would still be rotting on the street, worse than ever. She is my hero, my life's saviour.

Maria has improved her skills as well. At first she had much difficulty braiding *Wazungu* hair. "It's too silky and soft," she told Mrs. Scott. Mrs. Scott gave her wigs to practise on. Yes, there were frustrating moments. Maria once pulled the wig off the dummy's head and threw it on the floor. "Be gentle, dear," Mrs. Scott said in her usual calm voice. "That's the secret of success." She never lost patience with her.

With lots of practice, Maria has become a quick and confident *Muzungu* hair braider. Today, she is known as Mama Kiosk. There are brochures at the airport, tour centres, hotels and resorts with the picture of Mama

Kiosk braiding *Muzungu* hair. This brings many tourists to Freedom Kiosk. Mrs. Scott keeps a variety of beads for braiding. The most famous are the red earthy beads, handmade, irregular sizes and shapes, coarser than the factory-made, and also more expensive, but for the tourists still cheaper after converting dollars to shillings.

By the end of each day, I have made enough tips to buy myself some fruits and vegetables. Maria, on the other hand, makes an incredible amount on tips, enough to pick up a sack of rice or flour; she can also afford to buy oil and meat.

"These tourists are generous with tips," she says, counting her fortunes at the end of a shift, "not like Mama Fatima's customers used to be." She complains about *Wahindi* stinginess.

"But you miss Mama Fatima, don't you?" I ask her.

"I miss the *Muhindi* culture, very much so. We understand their language, eat their food, listen to their songs and laugh at their jokes. And the best part is, we enjoy it. Even our singers use Kiswahili lyrics to the Hindi movie tunes," she says with pride. "But with *Muzungu* we have to speak English and be diplomatic."

I laugh and pretend to speak like Mrs. Scott. "Good morning, Juma. What a splendid day." I cannot imitate the accent and make a total fool of myself.

Maria does not find humour in my stupidity and continues to be serious. "I suppose that's life. We move on just like they have." Maria will not admit that she misses

Mama Fatima. She asks Jena Bai, who looks much older and a lot fatter and waddles when she walks, if she has heard any news of Mama Fatima.

Jena Bai, in her terrible Kiswahili, complains, "*Wapi! Wao ni kupotea, bas. Wewe nani, mimi nani, kusahau kabisa.* Where! They are lost, that's it. Who are you, who am I? They forget completely."

A simple no is all Jena Bai needed to say. Maria and I have a good laugh, although not in front of her, God forbid.

As much as it hurts, we do understand why *Wahindi* are secretive about leaving the country. Their homes and businesses are valuable and in high demand, but if people know they are moving, then buyers wait until the departure date is close and come forward with the lowest offer, leaving them no choice but to sell out of desperation. Then there is the hassle with the porters, ticket agents, and customs officers, and especially with the airport clerks, who go through their bags, delaying them without reason. To avoid missing their flight, they pay an expensive *magendo*, bribe. None of this is worth it, so they keep the departure a secret and leave: no goodbyes, no hugs, no crying. A disheartening breakup, a relationship lost forever.

Maybe that is why we never knew that Mama Fatima was planning to go. Maria told me that Dada Zakiya was not aware of it either. When Mama Fatima received her visa, she kept it a secret until the last day and told Maria just as she was handing the keys to Mrs. Scott. I am sure Hamisi must have known. Like Dada Zakiya said, "Hamisi is more trusted than any of our friends or relatives. He is our *Dadabapa*, grandfather."

I plan to visit Hamisi once I have enough cash saved for the trip. Maria knows where his village is. I need to tell him the truth and clear my name—and find out how to contact Dada Zakiya.

party
august 1984

MRS. SCOTT ASKS Maria and me to be helpers at a barbeque party on Saturday for her husband's birthday. She speaks about her husband turning fifty to her friends and customers over and over again; it must be a magical number. I am going to be a server, or maybe a barbeque helper, Mrs. Scott is not sure yet. Everything will be finalized by Saturday afternoon. "I need one more female helper in the kitchen. Do you know anyone?" Mrs. Scott asks Maria.

I whisper to Maria, "How about Josephine?"

"Well, there is Josephine. She has an appointment today. I could ask her," Maria tells Mrs. Scott.

"That will be lovely. Juma will be happy to have her there." She gives me a nod as if asking for my approval.

When Josephine visits Maria for her weekly hair wash

and braiding, the bloody devil stands outside the door watching her, ensuring that she settles with Maria and has her braiding started. I do not greet Josephine or acknowledge her at all. He finally leaves Josephine alone and goes with Sophie, an orphaned fourteen-year-old he purchased over a year ago. Josephine had mentioned that Sophie was raped by her uncle the same night her parents died in a fatal bus accident. He sold her to the pimp within a week. As much as Josephine is sad about Sophie's fate, it makes her happy that the pimp splits his time between the two of them. This gives Josephine a bit of freedom.

"Special fresh coffee for you, my lady," I say and give the cup to Josephine. Maria winks at me.

Mrs. Scott smiles when I go to the counter to clear up some mess. "I know you fancy her. Why don't you ask her out?" she says. I avoid the question. Mrs. Scott is not aware of her profession, and I hope she never finds out.

Maria talks to Josephine about helping out at Mrs. Scott's party. "Oh no! I couldn't," she says. "That devil would kill me." But with a bit of persuasion, she agrees. "I will be there by two in the afternoon at the latest, if that is okay?"

"You may come here by twelve o'clock," Mrs. Scott says. "Maria has two clients booked in the morning. Then you can all catch a lift with me."

After paying, Josephine speaks to Maria. "I will find a way to escape and get there. If I am not here by twelve, then I will see you at Mrs. Scott's house."

I walk Josephine out of the kiosk. She looks around, making sure the pimp is not watching her. "Maybe I will not be able to escape," she says. "I am not sure why I agreed to help. And the beating I will take might not be worth it."

"Well then, you will just have to go home with me after the party, won't you?" I say. "Find a way to get there, then leave the rest to me. I will come prepared."

"Prepared?" She frowns.

"Run away! I have been asking you to run away since my freedom from the streets. I have a home now. Isn't it time you took that step?"

She shakes her head. "No, I can't. That devil will find us and kill us both. I can't." She runs towards the pole and waits for the pimp.

"Josephine, please," I say, walking towards her.

She raises her hand, signalling me to stop, and looks away. How beautiful she is. I hate those men who will mess her up tonight, I really hate them. Once again, with disappointment, I walk away from her and go back to work.

Josephine does not make it to the kiosk at twelve. We head to Mrs. Scott's house without her. "Do you think she will come?" Maria asks.

"I hope so," I say, although I doubt it.

Mrs. Scott honks by the closed gates of her house. The *askari* comes running, dressed in khaki shirt and trousers, his biceps bulging as he slides open two heavy iron gates. He could easily knock the pimp down, I think to myself. Just one blow, that would be enough. I wish I could tell Mrs. Scott to arrange it. The *askari* waves, and Mrs. Scott drives to the front of her huge mansion, which I bet could fit more than ten families from my neighbourhood. We stand on the driveway while she talks to the *askari*, who nods repeatedly. Two gardeners tending the front flowers and bushes keep busy with their work, paying no attention to our arrival. I have never seen such a clean residence.

"Wait here," Mrs. Scott says. "I will get Abdullah to settle you in your quarters. He is our head servant," and she goes into her house.

"Must be the shrimp money. This is a rich man's house for sure." Maria is as astonished as I am to see Mrs. Scott's lifestyle.

Mr. Scott owns a successful shrimp export business. He has big boats and hires expert fishermen to catch shrimp in the deep waters. The shrimp are sorted and cleaned at the processing plant, ready to pack and export as frozen food. I have heard he gives women first priority for jobs at the plant.

In a few minutes, a smart-looking man comes out of the house. "Hello, I am Abdullah," says the head servant.

"*Habari*, how are you?" Maria and I say together,

synchronized as though we had practised for months.

Abdullah asks us to follow him to the guest quarters, located at the back of the house, hidden behind the mango and guava trees. We pass a small toilet and shower room. Abdullah points at a boy sitting on a mat, studying. "This is my son. He is twelve and has to go to school on weekdays, Mrs. Scott's strict orders, so he is only a weekend helper at the house." His son stands up and greets us politely, and then goes back to his work. We carry on to the three rooms that make up the guest quarters. The biggest belongs to Abdullah, his wife and son. The other two, one for men and one for women, are used by the helpers who need to stay over from time to time. The rooms contain two bunk beds and a wooden cupboard filled with fresh uniforms and towels. "Sometimes we let our son use one of these rooms when it's empty. You know, a little private time for me and my missus," Abdullah says. Maria pretends she has not heard and settles her bag in the cupboard of the women's room.

The *askari* escorts another helper to the quarters, her face covered in a *kanga*, her breathing heavy. She drops the *kanga* and gives us a broad smile. "Victory!" Josephine says.

I can't believe it. "I didn't even recognize you," I say. "Look at you in *kanga* and . . ." I stop myself once I realize how excited I am and give her a hug.

"But you don't want to know how. This was not easy." Her hands shake, but she continues to smile.

"It doesn't matter now," I say, but I can only imagine the trouble she may have gone through. "The important thing is that you are here."

We follow Abdullah and meet the rest of the helpers at the poolside where lunch is being served. The back of this mansion is as magnificent as the front. Maria, Josephine and one more female helper hang around with Abdullah's wife, while I stay with the men. Josephine will have a great evening with Maria, I think, and maybe, just maybe, tomorrow I can convince her not to go back to him. She can be with me forever.

Luminous blue and red lights reflect from under the water of the swimming pool. Most of the young guests are in the pool, swimming laps, playing, diving and splashing water all around the tiled path. Towels are stacked evenly on the rack at the side of the pool area. Three couples dance on the veranda to soft music. The rest of the guests, seated at dinner tables in groups of eight scattered on the grass, chat and laugh.

The servers carry trays of special alcoholic drinks, making sure the party guests are well looked after. The spread of food on the long table is rich. I have never seen such colourful and decorative food in my life—all kinds of vegetables, fruits, potatoes, rice, bread and much more. Two barbeque cooks at the far end of the table, grilling the shrimp and other assorted meats, wear aprons with the number fifty printed on the front. I am wearing an ironed, white, Chinese-collared jacket over my t-shirt and black trousers. Mrs. Scott has a full collection of these uniforms in all different sizes. My job is to serve the barbeque to the guests as they order. The rest of the spread is self-serve.

This was Dada Zakiya's vision, to see me in a clean uniform, working as a waiter. Even though for only one night, I have done it. What a proud moment for me! If only Dada Zakiya were here to see me. I feel her spirit within me. I smile to myself and serve the barbeque. After dinner, all the helpers clean up while the party continues. The louder music begins, the dance floor livens up and colourful lights rotate over the guests, painting them in red, green, yellow, blue and purple. "Come on, darling, let's disco," one of the guests says to himself as he staggers away.

The female helpers in the kitchen wash the dishes and organize the serving of the dessert and coffee for later. Abdullah asks us to take our break. We serve ourselves the leftover food and settle at the side of the house under the gazebo to have our grand feast. Josephine and I sit next to each other. The variety of food delights my pallet. Every bite is tastier than the one before. I want the juicy shrimp to melt in my mouth forever. There is still much food left, and I cannot eat any longer. Never in my life did I think I would say *kashiba*, I've had enough, while there was still food offered to me. What an experience!

It is a perfect night. A full moon reflects on Josephine and her eyes sparkle. In her black dress with white frilled apron—unlike the revealing dresses she usually wears—and with barely any makeup on, her true beauty shines through. "I use Ponds," she told me once. In my opinion, she is a natural beauty; no *Muzungu* cream can make anyone as beautiful as her.

"I wish this was our full-time job," Josephine says.

"Dada Zakiya used to tell me that nothing is impossible. You can make it happen if you want to." I look straight into her eyes.

"I don't know how. I am scared."

"You have made it this far." I stroke her cheek. "Come stay with me for a while. Once you are free, you will know how." This time she smiles at me. I nod at her and she nods back.

"Okay, everyone." Abdullah claps twice. "Let's get back to work."

The next shift commences.

At past two in the morning, a handful of guests are still by the pool chatting with Mrs. Scott. Mr. Scott excused himself a while ago. The two night *askaris* give a nod to Abdullah after the safety check and go by the gated area for their night shifts. Abdullah walks us to the quarters to settle for the night.

"Good night," Maria says.

"I'm coming in a minute," Josephine says to Maria, and then to me she says, "I am terrified. What will happen to me tomorrow?" Her lips tremble.

"Do you trust me?" I ask. She looks down at the ground. "Just trust me, Josephine. I promise to keep you safe."

"This time he will kill me," she says.

"Go rest up. Tomorrow will be your new beginning. You will not regret it, I promise."

Without saying another word, Josephine joins Maria and the other women in their room. We are one too many men in our room. I volunteer to sleep on the terrazzo floor. With a pillow under my neck, I think of Josephine's escape. I know I am right to take her home with me. Even Dada Zakiya would want me to save and free her.

We gather outside the quarters under the tree for our morning tea. Abdullah reads each helper's name and hands us our envelopes. "Mrs. Scott has asked that you open it once you go home, please," he says. I kiss the envelope and stuff it in my shoe.

Abdullah's wife hands out pre-packed leftover food to each of us. Maria smells the bag, and I see saliva drool out of her mouth. Josephine laughs at her.

We are happy and ready to make our journey home. Mrs. Scott has arranged a taxi for Maria, Josephine and

me back to town. The driver first drops Maria at her
house and then both Josephine and me by the ferry berth.
Josephine, disguised as a village girl, has one *kanga*
wrapped over her dress and another covering her head
and mouth. I ask her not to speak till we board the ferry
so her voice will not be recognized. She runs to the toilet
and locks herself in. I wait outside for over thirty minutes
and then knock at the door. "Come on, Josephine, you
need to come out now," I say.

"No!" she says.

A woman waiting her turn knocks at the door harder.
"Finish it quick, or I will have to squat right at the doorstep."

Josephine comes out and runs towards the beach.
"This is a mistake, this a mistake," she repeats to herself.

"Look, you are creating a scene. Just be calm. Sit on
this log. It is okay." But in truth I am as scared as she is,
and every time someone passes by, I jerk, hiding my fear
to keep her calm. I hear a slight sigh of relief from her
when the ferry departs. The ocean wind blows over her
face, which she struggles to keep covered. I reach out and
remove the *kanga* from her face. She looks at me, unsure
whether I should have done that.

"Don't be afraid," I assure her, although I do not
know what would happen if he found us. This time I
would have to face him, be courageous, fight back.

She raises her head towards the clear blue sky and
welcomes the wind on her face with an even broader smile

than she had when she arrived at the party. For the first time, I see tears of happiness trickle down her cheek. She continues to smile for the rest of the ride. Yet her hands tremble. She grabs the edge of her *kanga*, unaware of her action, and twirls it around her finger. I grab her hand to remind her that I am here to protect her. The *kanga* unwraps from her finger. She relaxes and rests her head on my shoulder while I hold her by the waist. We stare at the ocean for the rest of the ride home.

Tonight we will toast Josephine's freedom.

magical kingdom
august 1984

"HERE WE ARE, Josephine," I say as we step off the ferry. "Did you ever imagine that one day you would be walking in this magical kingdom?"

"Magic?" she asks. "I hope so, because otherwise that devil will kill us."

"Not in my kingdom."

"What if?"

I pull a knife from my pocket and show it to her. "Like I said, not in my kingdom." She puts her hand on her mouth and gasps. "Whatever it takes," I say, and slide it back into my pocket.

I once moved here with Samuel for a better life, but I chose the wrong path and lost my freedom. Then again, I am grateful, because otherwise I would never have met Josephine, and she would not have stepped into my kingdom today. When I came back to search for Samuel after the watch incident, I found his hut abandoned, waiting for me to make it my home, giving me a second chance. Now no one can take this freedom away from Josephine and me, not anymore.

We walk overland in silence. I watch her being cautious of every person who passes by. She wraps her *kanga* back around her face. I do not say anything and let her be; my words will be meaningless today. I am confident that, in time, this move will bring her happiness and a better life, and she will feel that for herself.

Emanuel waits for my arrival by the entrance to my hut to hear all about the party. A fatherless child, he looks up to me as his mentor, big brother and entertainer. How well he has grown. At eleven, he is much taller than I was at that age. He runs to get Esta, calling out to his mother. I introduce Josephine to my wonderful neighbours.

Esta strokes Josephine's arm. "*Karibu*," she welcomes her. She takes Josephine's hand and walks her into my hut as though Josephine were a bride. We sit down on the mat and Emanuel settles next to me. For a moment there is an odd silence. Esta stares at Josephine. Normally, Esta is never wordless, but Josephine's beauty seems to have put a spell on her. Josephine forces a smile, so I ease the situation by getting food out of the bags.

We share the meal, and I tell Esta and Emanuel all

about the party, exaggerating some of it. We laugh about Mr. Scott being so drunk he could not even tell the difference between Mrs. Scott and the other ladies. He kissed every lady on the lips who had wished him a happy birthday. What a party! Emanuel is intrigued when I imitate the *Wazungu* dance. By the end of the evening, Josephine has relaxed and makes an effort at conversation. But I cut the gathering short. It has been a long day for Josephine. She needs her space and time to settle in her new home.

We set up a thick bedding blanket and lay it over the sisal mat on the brick floor by the stove for Josephine to sleep on. "This is too hard," she says, "and it is hot in here."

"You're most welcome to sleep in my room next to me on the foam mattress, if you wish." She takes the offer without hesitation. We pull down the mosquito net and tuck ourselves in. "I am sorry I cannot offer you any more comfort than this," I say.

"This is comfort," she says. "No more a sex slave. I will not allow any man to touch me ever again." She turns her face towards the wall.

"Sleep well, Josephine. You are free and this place is your heaven." I stroke her back. She stays silent.

I think of my first night on this mattress and how comfortable everything felt. But for Josephine, I know this is tough. She has been sleeping on spring beds in air-conditioned rooms. I lie sideways facing her and watch her curvy hips. I imagine stroking her body and getting closer to her, but I stop myself and pull away from the dream. "I will not allow any man to touch me ever again," she had said. I am not any man, I am her love. I will care for her, protect her and give her happiness. Perhaps in time, she will show me her affection. I know she feels the same for me as I do for her. It is her fear she must overcome.

In the middle of the night, I hear Josephine crying. I get her some water. She sits up. Her tears roll down uncontrollably as she sips the water. I put the glass aside and wipe her tears with my hands, but she stops me. "Let them run their course. They have been accumulating for too long."

I kiss her forehead. "I will kill him before he does anything to you. I swear to that."

She smiles, feeling safe, and the tears dry up. Shortly after, she goes to sleep. My Josephine, sweet Josephine. I watch her for hours till I cannot keep my eyes open any longer.

pimp
august 1984

THE PIMP SHOWS up at the kiosk the next day. He greets Mrs. Scott and asks to talk to Maria. "*Jambo*," Maria says.

The pimp moves close to Maria. "Do you know where Josephine is? She has been missing since Saturday." He stares at her as though he is reading her mind. "She was here for her hair braiding last Thursday. Is there anything she told you that I should know?"

Maria, thank heavens, realizes that Josephine never went back to the pimp. She responds without hesitation, "Well," and steps back a bit. "I remember her mentioning that her rich customer had offered to take her to the northern region and promised her a luxurious life. I hope that helps. But I am sorry; I wasn't paying much attention to exactly where and when." She pauses for a moment. "Oh yes, I remember her spending some time at the textile store. Maybe the shopkeeper knows something."

The pimp squints but Maria politely goes back to her customer. He barges out of the kiosk and grabs Sophie's arm, pulling her roughly across the street, and goes to the textile store.

"What's going on?" Maria asks when we eat our lunch at the back of the kiosk. I tell Maria everything. She promises not to speak to anyone about Josephine's whereabouts, knowing that this is a matter of life and death for her.

A week later, the pimp drops Sophie off for hair braiding and stands outside by the pole watching her. Sophie has never had her hair done before. Her bruised eye says a lot. She speaks softly and asks tricky questions about Josephine. The pimp does not budge from the pole during the entire braiding session. Maria sticks to her promise and stays quiet as though she is oblivious to what is happening. I carry on with my cleaning, not paying any interest but hoping this will be the first and last time that Sophie visits us and that we never see either of them ever again. But I am wrong. The pimp waits outside the kiosk at closing time.

"Be careful," Maria tells me.

The pimp follows me, staying a good ten steps behind. I am afraid. Please, God, don't let him find out. Give me courage. What to do? I change direction and walk towards the slums, confidently, as if I know where I am heading. I stop to watch children playing in the mud. I go

to a stall where a woman is frying *mogo* chips and buy a
packet. Not that I wish to spend money, but I have to
slow down the process of going nowhere. But the pimp is
still behind me. I walk to another woman standing
outside her corrugated tin shack, smoking, skinny, no
flesh left on her. I talk to her, making sure the pimp
cannot hear us, and we negotiate a price. She invites me
into her dump, which smells worse than the trash in the
area, as fowl as a chicken coop. She prepares me tea and
offers a biscuit, and allows me to sleep for the night.

"So pay me," she says.

"In the morning," I say. I stay up all night, worried
about Josephine. She must be devastated. I pray, pray,
pray.

The next day is a tough, long day. Once again, the
pimp waits outside the kiosk at closing. Damn it! I sweat
like hell. This goes on for the next three days. I borrow an
advance from Mrs. Scott and pay the slum woman, who is
kind enough to make me *ugali* on the third day. On the
fourth day, I have had enough of this chase. No more, I
say to myself. I turn back and walk towards him. We
stand face to face staring at each other. I do not blink, not
even once. I swiftly pull the knife from my pocket and
push him into the gulley against the wall. Surprised, he
does not fight but manages his usual intimidating
language. "What the fuck!"

I lean against him, with the knife at his neck. "You do
not fuck me," I say in the same harsh voice. I stoop to his

level, to be just like him. My heart races like a stampede and sweat drips down my forehead. "Do not follow me," I say as loud as if he were a deaf man. I feel the wetness of his blood on my palm and see that I have scratched him. "I do not like you, I do not like the way you look, I do not like the way you smell, and I do not like what you do in your life. Do not follow me or come anywhere near me again. Now get out of my sight!" and I release the knife from his neck before I am tempted to cut him to pieces. His tough body shrinks away from me, but his eyes are more terrifying than ever. I walk away as fast as I can. A street later I run, looking behind me a few times to make sure he is not following me. Just in time, I make the ferry to go home.

My entire body shakes. I take a deep breath, allowing the ocean breeze to calm me down. Suddenly, Esta appears next to me in the ferry. Without words, she holds her hands in a prayer position and gives me a smile. Emanuel hugs me tight, wrapping his arms around my waist, and cries.

"It's okay, it's okay," I say and release Emanuel from the hug, though I am in no mood to talk.

"Your friend Josephine has been crying," he says. "I was giving her company at night. I don't know why she thinks you might be dead."

I rub his head. "Have you been doing your homework? Just because I am supposed to be dead doesn't mean you don't study," I say, changing the subject.

"Yes, I have. I've been a good boy," he says.

"Good, that's the way it should be."

We stay quiet and watch the ripples created by the departing ferry. I exhale.

Josephine clings to me, her body pressing against mine like a magnet. No words said. Then she slaps me. "Where have you been?" she cries. "Do you have any idea how worried I have been?"

I can only imagine the fear she has lived through these last four days. "I am here and I am not going anywhere, okay?" I assure her. She grins, and then lets out a perfect cry, like lost love found and we live happily ever after, like the Hindi movies or the fairy tales Dada Zakiya used to read to me, where the prince always rescues the princess in the end. But I know this is not the end and this is not a fairy tale.

She walks away towards the kitchen. "We need to talk," she says.

I sigh. "I need a wash, and then we shall talk." I pick up a bucket filled with water standing by the entrance and head out to the facilities. It was rough and smelly in the slums, and the anxiety of getting home, worrying about Josephine and confronting the pimp is draining. Now I am here, back in my kingdom, taking a good wash with the perfumed soap—Imperial Leather—that Mrs. Scott gave me last month. The bar is much smaller than it was a week ago, which reminds me that I have a woman living in my hut and enjoying the luxuries I have in my possession.

The scrub is uplifting, and washing my knife is even more uplifting. I cannot believe that I fought that bastard. Where did the courage come from? All I knew was that I had to end it and get back home to Josephine. I promised her freedom and happiness, and I will do anything to protect her. I look at my reflection in the pocket mirror and give myself an approving nod. Now I need to convince Josephine that he is a bloody coward who intimidates those smaller than him. He bullies young girls and hurts *only* them, but she is a tigress and he cannot touch her. The mirror slips from my hand, creating a perfect crack, a line right in the middle. I check my reflection in the cracked mirror and laugh, amazed how courageous and strong I look from both sides of the crack. "I fought the bastard!" I say aloud and laugh more.

I head back in the direction of my hut with an empty bucket and think of Emanuel, how hard he works bringing me buckets full of water from the water pipe. Before going to my hut, I knock at Esta's. "*Karibu,*" she answers. Emanuel, happy to see me, runs and gives me a hug, the same emotional hug he gave me on the ferry.

"I am not going to die," I tell him. "I want you to know that I will always be here for you."

"Why did she think you might be dead?" Esta asks.

I smile. "Maybe someday I can explain, but all is fine,"

I say. "See you tomorrow. And thank you for taking care of Josephine while I was away. You are a kind boy." I look right into Emanuel's eyes. "Tomorrow evening, we will read a book together." Emanuel gives me a thumbs up and smiles.

Josephine is silent while I tell her the pimp incident in detail. Deep in her own thoughts, she prepares a warm drink of *uji*, cream of wheat, for us. I sit on the floor with legs criss-crossed and watch her. She seems confused, not sure whether to cry or laugh. She tells me she is more scared than ever, but I assure her he will not harm us, ever.

"I have to go back," she says and hands me a cup of *uji*. "You have your own dreams. You have freed yourself from the street life. Here you are today, with a good home and a good job. These are the beginnings of your dreams and I am shattering them, putting you in danger all over again. You were lucky this time, that's all. I must go."

"My life is incomplete without you," I say. I put my drink on the floor and hold her hand. She looks down, shaking her head. I want to kiss her luscious lips, to complete myself, but she stands up and turns away, her back towards me.

I know how to be romantic. I think of the Hindi movie Dada Zakiya took me to on a hot afternoon in an air-conditioned theatre. We munched on *jugu* and drank cold Coca-Cola as we watched *Raj Babar* sing a love song to *Ranjeeta*. Dada Zakiya kept singing the song after the movie. She laughed at me when I tried. I still remember the song: *tu istara se meri zindagi me shamil he, jaha bi jahu ye lagta he teri mehfil he*. I sing it to Josephine and she turns to me, laughing. I cannot express my feelings with words anymore. She stands still, unsure of my intention. I reach her lips and give her a soft kiss. Then I wait for her approval. She smiles at me and moves much closer, breathing heavily, her chest pumping. With my hands wrapped around her ears, we indulge in a passionate kiss. I feel her, touch her. I pick her up and take her to the bedroom. She removes her dress and stands in front of me in a soft cotton petticoat—a pink petticoat—and the colour against her skin enhances her beauty. She has developed into a most beautiful woman, tall, with big bosoms and curvy hips. A slight wetness trickles between her breasts. She undresses. Her soft naked body brushes against mine, and we make love.

nightmares
october 1984

JOSEPHINE PLACES CUT-UP leaves in a coffee tin and displays the garnish in the centre of the mat where we sit to eat our dinner. She dims the lantern, adding a romantic ambiance, but there is sadness in her eyes. Despite all the love I give her, and a home she can call a *home*, she lives in fear, a fear I cannot afford to have. I stay brave for both of us and make her a promise that her life will be full of laughter and happiness and free from worries. But it is not easy for her, especially when the devil lives in her thoughts.

The biggest worry is the nightmares; Josephine has one episode every night. It is always him, finding her, cutting her up into pieces. She presses her chest. "It hurts," she says, and then has difficulty breathing. Sometimes she has tremors and sweats. I splash water on her face to cool her down. Many times she is nauseous. The best way to comfort her is to hold her against my chest, letting her hear my heart vibrating against her ear, reminding her that we are still here, breathing, alive and together.

Recently, the early mornings have been the best time for Josephine, all praise to Esta, I must say. Josephine prepared her favourite *vitumbua*, rice cake patties—learned from her mother when she was little—and invited Esta and Emanuel to join us. "This is delicious," Esta said. "How about you cook up some fresh ones tomorrow morning and I can have Kanji Bhai sample them. If he likes them, you can sell them to him and make a bit of money."

Kanji Bhai accepted, and since then, Josephine has joined Esta in her kitchen at five every morning to cook. Josephine makes a little money from her cooking, but what matters most to her is the happiness she feels.

Josephine wakes me up and talks about the excitement of spending time with Esta. "She is the mother I wish I had," she says. "Emanuel is a lucky child." She makes the best hot black tea for me, and we share one *kitumbua*.

"True, but it breaks my heart not to see him go to school."

"I know, but you can't change the whole world." She gives me a soft kiss on my lips and tickles my underarm. "Juma, the saviour."

I hold her close. "Have a blessed day, love," I say. I see the sadness return to her eyes as she stands by the entrance waving goodbye. I ask God to take care of her while I am gone, and head out with Esta and Emanuel to catch the ferry to town.

For the rest of the day, Emanuel stays with Esta at their vendors' spot selling boiled eggs. I have tried to reason with Esta. Emanuel should be at school, but she refuses, claiming she needs his help. Now, that is outrageous, but I have no say in this. So instead I teach him to read and write like Dada Zakiya taught me. We go to the library together and borrow some fun books.

Every Sunday, Emanuel picks up the empty buckets from the women's huts further from the water pipe and fills them up for ten cents each. This Sunday, one of the women tricks him. After all his effort, she refuses to pay him more than five cents. Left with no choice, he takes the five cents and then pours half the water out of the bucket. The woman is mad at him. Emanuel sticks out his tongue and makes a grunting sound to shut her up. The rest of the women dare not pay him less.

He is an expert at carrying multiple buckets at a time, two on each arm and one balanced on his head. I can manage only one in each hand, and it takes me twice as long to walk back to my hut. In the meantime, Emanuel has made a second round with more water for me, since I have to share with Josephine.

"Now you have to charge me," I say.

"You are my brother," he says. "Families don't charge each other." When I insist, he stops me from reaching into his pocket but I manage to drop a coin. He stays quiet.

Later in the afternoon, Emanuel and Josephine play marbles in the sand for hours. I grab one of the books from the library and get comfortable, seated against the entrance of my hut. Every so often, I glance at Josephine, especially when she screams in victory, striking the marble perfectly into the circle. She becomes like a child, giggling and jumping, and wins the game. In the evening, Emanuel visits and shows me his homework. We study for a while and I read him a story. Josephine cuddles next to me and enjoys our storytime together.

"Thank you for being my tutor," Emanuel says, slamming the coin into my palm. "For your services."

"All right, you've proved your point."

I promise that I shall treat him as my brother and understand that families do not charge each other. He laughs and boasts about his speedy water service. "With some practice you will be as good as I am." I smack his butt and tell him to get out of here. Josephine bursts into laughter. If only she stayed happy and content all the time. Unfortunately, the sun sets, we go to sleep, and once again the nightmares begin.

Three months pass and Josephine's *kitumbua* business is short-lived—and so too my luxurious breakfasts. Inflation is high and it is impossible to buy rice. The ration shops

hide rice, oil and flour, reserving it mostly for *Wahindi*—
at a very high price. Jena Bai, for example, has a never-
ending supply for her restaurant. Esta has a tough time
maintaining her profits from the *mandazi* business, even
though she manages to buy white flour from the supplier
who has known her for years. Kanji Bhai takes advantage
of the situation and increases the price of *mandazi* while
refusing to pay any extra to Esta. There is a shortage of
corn flour for *ugali*, but luckily Maria knows farmers
from the village.

Once again I borrow money from Mrs. Scott, more
than I can pay back. She deducts ten percent from my
salary, and twice she has pardoned me and cleared the
debt to zero. "This time, I am not lending it for free. No
debt will be pardoned," she says.

Depending on my tips, I purchase vegetables and
fruits. Sometimes Mrs. Scott buys fruits from the vendors
passing by the kiosk and shares them with Maria and me.
I wish she would purchase chicken for us, but I think the
sight of the vendor holding live chickens upside down
upsets her—I cannot understand why—and she rudely
tells the vendor to leave. The best part of working for Mrs.
Scott is the free coffee I get to drink and the imported
biscuits. Though the package reads Butter Shortbread, it
is not bread. I often take two biscuits and save one for
Josephine. Every Monday, at the end of my shift, I pick
up beef bones for Mrs. Scott's dogs from the butcher,
who keeps scraps of meat for me, mostly fat but with

some meat. I take one of the bones and drop it in my bag; I do not think the dogs will mind. Josephine prepares a delicious beef soup with vegetables and *ugali*, a festive Monday. At the end of our meal, we take turns sucking the bone marrow until it is completely dry, to the point where even the dogs would refuse to have it. For the rest of the week, we eat *ugali* with spinach and carrots.

Although the pimp has not come to visit me since our last incident, or sent Sophie back for hair braiding, I do not take anything for granted and stay alert at all times, especially after work when I head to the ferry. But today I hear the best news from one of the night ladies when she comes to Maria for hair braiding. In the middle of telling us the night-street gossip, she mentions the pimp. After all these months, he has finally given up his search for Josephine in the city. He has packed his bags and moved to the northern region with Sophie, convinced that he will find Josephine there. I rejoice with a smile. "Oh Mama Kiosk, that man has gone mad," the night lady says. "It was bound to happen—luck would strike her at some point in her life. Josephine was too beautiful. Let's hope she is happy wherever she is and he never finds her. But sadly, one's bad luck is the price of another's good luck."

"How do you mean?" Maria continues braiding her hair.

"Well, his new commodity, Sophie, has to put up with his anger," the night lady says, shaking her head. "He is not nice when he is angry. That poor girl. Mchh! What to do!" After the customer leaves, Maria claps my hand in victory. I cannot wait to share the good news with Josephine that she has nothing to fear from the pimp. She is now free—the devil has moved.

Maria is almost done with her customer. The kiosk quietens and I am getting ready for my lunch break. Mrs. Scott, as usual, goes to the phone to chat with her friends, and drops half her sandwich. "My goodness! Never fails." She picks up the sandwich from the floor and throws it in the dustbin.

I rush to rescue her. "I will clean it up." As I pretend to clean up the scattered pieces of cheese and tomato from the floor by the dustbin, I grab the leftover sandwich—quicker than a mouse—and stuff it in my pocket. Yes, that night lady was right: one's bad luck is the price of another's good luck. Maria rolls her eyes. I stick out my tongue and pat my heart.

I sit outside on the footpath and wipe the dirt off the sandwich—mostly just bread with a small piece of cheese. I eat it with the *maharagwe* that Josephine has packed for my lunch, and I think of her. I imagine her doing the same, thinking of me as well, as she takes her break from the daily chores. Maybe she has washed my shirt and hung it over the tree branch to dry. Then she will go for a walk before joining the elderly ladies for a wisdom chat. I cannot wait to get home and give her the great news about the devil. I am hopeful that, now, Josephine's nightmares will vanish.

"He is a devil. I cannot believe he would give up so easily. Something is not right," Josephine says at bedtime. "Shh! I hear him. He is here. Hide, quick."

"There is no one here, love." I say. "I have told you, he has gone to the northern region. It's been almost four months now. He is not coming back. I am sure he has moved on and settled in a new street, a new life. And so should you."

"No, he is back, hiding, wanting me to believe he is gone so he can catch me." She truly feels his presence, sees him. He haunts her memories, and his silence torments her. She tenses her body in fear. I hold her close, twenty minutes at least, till she falls asleep.

As the days go by, the nightmare becomes worse. It is as if it has become her state of being. She does not see the world as it is, only him, and she locks herself in the hut, refusing to do anything. I try to feed her, but she pushes the food away. I do not know what to do. I speak to Sushmita, the doctor's assistant. After all these years, Sushmita still rescues me by snitching medicine from the doctor's cupboard, for headache, tummy ache, nausea, malaria, whatever I need. But this is big; she is not sure of the diagnosis. Later, when the doctor leaves the dispensary, she brings me a small brown envelope. "I can only sneak five or the doctor will know." She gives me a sympathetic look. "I am not sure if I should be giving you such strong tablets. Anyway, try them out. Give her one every night, and remember, I have not given you these, so keep it quiet."

"What are these?"

"Valium. It will make her happy, I think. From my observation, the patients who used to cry all the time are much happier when they start this medication. Just try it."

As usual, I offer to do her chores, or anything, to help her. Instead, she asks me to pray for her that the third child she is carrying is a boy. Her two daughters have brought much misery to her marriage. If she disappoints the family this time, her mother-in-law has threatened another wife for her son.

I get home exhausted. Josephine is lying on the mattress and does not acknowledge me. I cook up some *ugali* with spinach and ask her to join me. She comes out of the room. "Look at me!" She is angry. "Just look at this." She pinches her face and her voice becomes demanding. "I am ugly, dry skin, no Ponds to use, and stuck in this prison."

I sit next to Esta by her hut. I am not sure if I should ask for her advice, but she knows, she hears us. Josephine is a loud girl, and when she is angry she gets even louder, sometimes on purpose. This has got her into trouble many times. We would be hiding from the pimp, but her voice would always give her away. But then, when it came time to confront the pimp, she would be silent, as if she were torturing him.

Emanuel stays busy, looking through his book, while Esta pats my back to comfort me, or maybe to sympathize. I need her guidance. My stomach churns in pain, a sensation I have been experiencing a lot lately.

"Maybe it is none of my business," Esta says, "but I think she is either a spoilt rich girl or she is mad."

"She is not mad," I say in her defence, "and she is not a spoilt rich girl. She had many luxuries in her previous life, but what was the point? She was not happy."

"She doesn't seem happy with you either. Take her out sometime. She is isolating herself in that tiny hut, locking herself up. This may cure her. At least do it before the next full moon." Esta and her superstitious beliefs.

All I want is happiness and freedom for Josephine, not isolation. The medication calms her, sedates her, and she sleeps undisturbed. I, too, have a restful night.

Three days later, she appears happier, cooking, allowing me to hold her and make love to her. Two more Valiums left, then what? I look up at the sky, seeking an answer. Stars glitter around the crescent moon, reminding me of the Diwali festivals and the happiness the sparks of light bring to people. That is what I need to bring back to Josephine's life—sparks! Esta is right. It is time to take her somewhere and glitter her with joy and laughter.

journey
may 1985

I ADMIT THAT Mrs. Scott is tough and firm when it comes to work, but she is also the most generous person. And I am blessed to be working for her. She hands me an envelope with extra wages for my one-week vacation. "Thank you, Mrs. Scott," I say, and whistle.

She smiles, opens the cash register and gives me an additional one hundred shillings. "You've earned it," she says with a naughty grin, winking at Maria as though she is being mischievous, planning to take it all away. But she does not, and the bonus is mine to keep. Now I can afford to purchase two bus tickets to visit Hamisi's village, as well as make my vacation a more pleasant and luxurious trip. It is high time I met Hamisi, and taking Josephine on this important journey will do us both good. I have not been completely fair with her. I have taken her for granted, believing that moving her into my home would give her freedom, when in fact it isolated her. The vacation will give her a chance to fight her demons. She needs to experience for herself the freedom of going to town, being safe. What is the point of living in fear? You may as well not live at all, because life is more than that. I truly believe that if we keep our love alive and be each other's strength, we can face our pain and suffering, and move forward.

I hold Josephine's hand. "Close your eyes. I have a surprise for you," I say. Then I place the tickets in her hand.

She opens her eyes. "What is this?"

"Tomorrow to Hamisi's village we go."

"I can't. That devil will find me." Her hands tremble and she drops the tickets.

"He is not coming back, Josephine. Maria asked one of the night ladies and that's what she told her." I kiss her forehead. "I need you, my love. I can't face Hamisi by myself. Don't you want to get away from here? I am doing this for you, too."

"I can't." She looks away.

I hold her tight. "I wouldn't do this if I knew you weren't safe, huh." I bribe her with half the bonus. "You can buy whatever you want from the city."

This time she smiles, grabs the money and hugs me.

"Ponds, I will buy Ponds." She runs to give Esta the news.

I stand in the middle of the room by myself, wondering if it was genuine care for me that convinced her—or the fifty shillings. Is she my true life partner, my love, my support when I need her the most? Doubt bothers me.

The next morning, Josephine shows no fear, no anxiety, and makes no mention of the pimp. She whistles while she packs her extra clothing, laying it in the middle of one of her *kanga*, then folding the *kanga* and tying it into a knot. She hums a happy tune, kisses the fifty shillings and tucks it into her bosom. In the meantime, I pack my stuff in a *kikapu* together with our meal.

When we reach the town, Emanuel pleads with us to take him. With much effort, Esta convinces him that I will take him the next time. I promise him that it will be a special journey, just him and me, which both Esta and I know will never happen. It is one of the many shattered dreams he will face as life goes by, but at this moment he is happy, happy to have a dream. He shakes my hand, gripping it tightly as though binding our promise, and then heads off in a run towards Kanji Bhai's teashop. "*Safari njema.*" Esta wishes us a safe trip and runs to catch up with him. Josephine and I take a different route, to the *sokoni*.

Covered in her *kanga*, Josephine walks closer to me, brushing her arms against mine as though seeking safety, making sure I am here to protect her. I put her hand to my lips and kiss it. We purchase fruits for the journey and then queue up at the bakery for almost an hour, hoping the baker will not run out of bread. Bread is a rare find these days, with only two bakeries left in the city. It is not a good choice of business anymore. During these tough times, bread has been rationed to only one loaf per family, at a fixed price. Bribing, however, is everywhere, and many customers walk out with two or three loaves, which means extra money in the baker's pocket and no bread for some of the people in the queue. I pray, "Please God, let there be one last loaf left for me."

Finally, with nine customers ahead of us, we step into the narrow bakery. The shelves are empty. The cashier pushes the back door open and sticks her head out, screaming at the sweaty workers kneading the dough— spread on the floor—with their feet. "*Haraka! Haraka!* Hurry! Hurry!" For another thirty minutes, we wait. Then, with the fresh, warm, sweet-smelling bread put away in the *kikapu*, we go to the Indian store to pick up some spices for Hamisi—*elchi*, cardamom; *jeera*, cumin; *luving*, cloves; and *tuj*, cinnamon. I want to buy some *kesar*, saffron, for biryani rice, but it is too expensive.

Outside the Indian store, Josephine stops on the footpath and glances around. "The devil is gone, truly gone! You were right." She swings my hand and drops her *kanga* off her face, allowing herself to be exposed for everyone to admire. It feels great to see her confidence return and the fear leave her body. She stands straight and tall, with great pride, and takes a giant step forward, freedom written all over her. This time, I do not hold her hand. Instead, I put my own hand in my pocket and grab hold of the knife, keeping it ready—just in case.

Two hours later, exhausted from our long walk in the heat, we collapse on the bench at the bus depot. I look around thoroughly, making sure the pimp is not here. Now out of her isolation, Josephine is happy, energetic, without fear. I let her enjoy the mood, even though deep inside I feel pain. How could I have made her a prisoner? Did she mean it? Would she rather be the devil's prisoner? She smiles at me, as if reading my thoughts and assuring me that it is not true—and that she is happy with me.

We share the boiled potatoes Josephine prepared for lunch and eat a banana each. Josephine rests her head on her *kanga* pack and falls asleep. The annoying flies buzz around my ears and tickle my arms. I stay awake, irritated, fighting the damn flies, yet keenly aware of our surroundings.

Close to seven at night, we check into bus number five, taking a spot at the back of the bus. Four *Wahindi* girls take the row in front of us and talk excitedly about the safari they are planning with friends from another town. I laugh at their jokes and whisper in Josephine's ear. The couple next to us pay no attention.

"You understand everything *Wahindi* say?" Josephine asks.

"Yes, and I should. After all, my Dada Zakiya spoke this Kutchi language."

"I am sure Hamisi does too," she says.

"He can also cook *Wahindi* meals. I am looking forward to meeting him and tasting his food again."

We eat boiled eggs and part of our precious loaf of bread. The *Wahindi* girls feast on their meal, and the aroma brings back memories of Dada Zakiya. They entertain the entire bus with their songs. The couple next to us, still in their own thoughts, skip dinner.

Around eleven, we reach our first stop, a small town. The *Wahindi* girls pull the toilet rolls out of their bags and run for the facilities. Locals in the bus laugh. "Delicate, too delicate," one of them says. "*Aaah, lakini*, true, but entertaining, *kabisa heh*, no doubt," another says.

Josephine, reluctant to leave the bus, covers her face. I once again assure her safety and purchase one stick of *mishkaki* and one *matoke* from the barbeque vendor, and we share a bottle of Fanta.

At midnight, the bus driver dims the lights and asks everyone to be quiet. Josephine falls asleep on my shoulder. Around three in the morning, we reach another rural town and are amazed at how quickly the vendors line up. "It seems like they schedule their time according to the bus hours," Josephine says and walks out of the bus for a stretch, this time completely confident of her freedom.

The bus driver rests by the chai *banda*, drinking hot tea to keep himself awake. "How many more stops before we reach our destination?" I ask him.

"It is about a one-hour drive through the rural housing in this area. I pick up locals and drop them wherever they wish. It is a pay-as-you-go deal. You know, *chini chini*, under the table. I have to feed my children, too, you know." He sips his tea. "*Halafu moja kwa moja*, and then straight to our destination."

"*Sawa*, for sure," I say.

Despite the darkness, the driver keeps the lights on now, and the passengers pay on their way out according to the distance. Suddenly, a pick-and-drop passenger rushes to the rear door and forces it open, jumping out of the bus before it stops. The other passengers seated at the rear scream in shock. The driver slams on the brake, bringing the bus to a screeching stop. "Did someone just jump off the bus?" he asks in disbelief, getting out of his seat before finishing his sentence.

Everyone is wide awake now. Josephine clings to the window, checking to see if she can spot the escaping man, but it is too dark. Three men and I run to the road with the driver. Sure enough, a few metres away, the man is bleeding from a head injury. A passenger helps the driver pick him up and put him on the floor of the bus. The driver reverses the bus and announces that he has to take the injured man, screaming in agony, with blood pouring out of his head, back to the rural town for help. Another passenger, a nurse, wraps a scarf around his head and lays his head on a pillow that one of the *Wahindi* girls hands to her, holding him tight to stop the bleeding.

"So much for trying to make extra money," the driver says. "Maybe I should have left him on the road."

"I wish such an incident to happen to the devil, that's what he deserves," Josephine says in an evil voice. I squeeze her hand tight and stay quiet, and she holds my hand as though knowing that deep in my heart I feel the same.

At the town, the driver stops at the police station and takes a long time talking to the police. The nurse is upset. "He needs medical attention. We need a doctor, not the damn police," she says.

The policeman comes into the bus and looks at the injured man. "*Aya ya ya, bahati mbaya!* bad luck!" he says, shaking his head. He goes back to his small office and continues talking the driver. Finally, he returns to the bus. "I am sorry for taking so long but we need the whole story, you know. I have to write down the statement from the driver and I need one witness signature." I raise my hand and volunteer. "Okay, follow me," he says. "By the way, does anyone have a pen so I can write down the statement?" A sigh of disbelief echoes through the bus. Someone finds a pen.

After nearly an hour, two policemen pick up the injured man for medical attention. At least I hope so. The driver slams the door shut and drives off at high speed, ranting on and on about how much time the policeman wasted. The nurse breaks down in tears, and the four *Wahindi* girls try to soothe her. "I am a nurse, I save people," she says. "I could not do much because of that policeman."

"Yes! They wanted a bribe," the driver explains. "I told them they could let him die and keep his body. I am paying them nothing."

Now everyone is quiet. The driver has dimmed the lights and we are on our way to Hamisi's village.

village
may 1985

JOSEPHINE AND I walk for almost an hour, away from the main highway on the country road heading to the village. I take a fistful of the rich, red soil and feel its energy, as though the earth here is happier. Despite the hot day, with the sun directly above us, the country air is fresh and clean. It does not smell like the city, like the fumes of car exhaust. Already I like it here.

We come across women with baskets on their heads. "*Jambo*," Josephine says. "How far before we reach the village?"

"*Hapo hapo tu*, just around the corner," one of the women says.

We pick up our pace in excitement, knowing we will soon be there. We walk close behind the women, but they begin to walk faster and eventually disappear out of sight.

An hour later, we have still not reached the village, and we wonder what *just around the corner* really meant to those women. Josephine comes to a full stop. "That's it, no more." She sits down and we take a rest.

Josephine lifts her face skyward, taking a sip of the last bit of water in the bottle, and I admire her long neck. Despite her exhaustion, she is beautiful. I remember her standing by the pole at her night job. No matter how tired she was, she never failed to look beautiful for her next customer. I stop myself in disgust. How could I think about her beauty and her night job at the same time? I ask my deep spirit to forgive me, and get up abruptly and walk away.

"I am too tired. I want to rest." Josephine calls me back.

I avoid her and keep walking. She runs after me. We walk for a while and then I break the silence. "There it is." I point downward to the village, and before I know it she is running downhill and I am trying to catch up with her.

One of the *mzee*, old man, calls us. "*Ume potea wapi?* Where are you, lost?"

"*Shikamo.*" I greet him respectfully while trying to catch my breath. Josephine bows to him.

He nods. "*Sema*, what's up?"

"Sorry to disturb you. We are looking for Hamisi," I say.

"Hamisi? *Aaahh*, I will take you to him.

"*Ahsante sana,*" Josephine says.

How do you know him?" he asks.

"We are relatives," I say.

"*Karibu.*" He welcomes us to the village and takes us to Hamisi's home, a cozy home made of bricks, twice the size of my hut, with a wooden door at the entrance. The *mzee* leaves us by the doorstep. I freeze, as though my blood has stopped circulating. Josephine holds my hand to comfort me. "*Hodi.*" I knock on the door, asking for a permission to enter.

Hamisi comes to the door gracefully, but soon his attitude changes. He frowns and his nostrils swell in irritation. Good lord, I think to myself. It has been such a long time and here he is, angry and upset, no, actually disgusted, just like he was the last time I saw him, at the doorstep of Dada Zakiya's flat. He puts his hands in the air and sighs as though questioning God. Why? But this time, I am not leaving without making a truce with him.

"Baba Hamisi," I say, "I have come a long way." He turns away, waving me goodbye, shaking his head.

Josephine steps forward. "Maria sends her greetings," she says. Hamisi turns towards her, surprised. "Baba Hamisi, Juma has been working with Maria all this time. It was a huge misunderstanding. You need to know that."

Hamisi sighs softly and lets us in. He settles on a foot-high wooden stool. Josephine settles on the other stool and I sit criss-crossed on the mat in front of them.

"*Ahsante.*" My hands shake, so I tuck my palms under

my thighs, though my voice may give my nervousness away. "Baba. May I call you Baba? Dada Zakiya told me you were like a grandfather to her, so may I?"

"Zakiya, Zakiya, Zakiya," he says, rubbing his chest. "My child. I wonder whatever happened to her." He clears his throat.

We have a long chat. I explain everything and he tells me everything. By the end, Josephine is crying more than the two of us. Hamisi and I hug each other. "How rude of me," he says. "I have not even offered you a glass of water." Josephine goes with him to the clay water pot and helps him serve the water. We give him all the Indian spices. He sniffs each packet, laughing and crying at the same time.

The next day, Hamisi shows us his small *shamba* at the back of his home, where he grows spinach and onions. He has many chickens roaming free. "With God's will, the weather has been cooperating. Last season was too dry. The rains didn't pour as much as we wished," he says. "I lost a couple of chickens in the heat. Mchh! That still saddens me."

He passes me some corn feed to throw to the chickens. "It is difficult, but I am blessed with youngsters in the village who respect me and come to me for advice. They provide me offerings. What more can an old man ask for, heh?" He picks up fresh chicken eggs and prepares us a luxurious breakfast, calling it Dadima's style *putlo*. "An Indian omelette that Dadima used to cook on Sundays," Hamisi says.

Josephine wondered about his family, but I asked her not to mention it. Dada Zakiya told me that he lost his wife and child during birthing complications, and never wishes to talk about it. He never married again, dedicating his life instead to Dada Zakiya's family. Maria is his distant family, but he does not talk much of his relatives.

After breakfast, Hamisi shows us the village. At the well, both Josephine and I are mesmerized by the effortless flow of clean water. "My! My! This well would be nice in our neighbourhood," Josephine says.

I think of Emanuel and wish he were here. His mouth would fall open. He would probably hug the flowing water and never let it go. I pull out a small notebook and pencil from my trousers pocket and make a quick sketch so Emanuel can see what it looks like.

"It was part of the foreign aid to prevent a further cholera outbreak," Hamisi says. "The villagers and foreigners worked together to build this gift for us."

"Yes, I have heard of this project. It was one of the successful projects set up in many villages," I say.

"Now we need a good clinic," Hamisi says. "It takes us too long to get to the doctor. It is difficult to take such a long journey to the hospital when one is sick. Premature deaths can be prevented."

"Dada Zakiya spoke of this." I am so excited that I

almost tell them the entire ten-year plan she came up with.

"Big talk." Hamisi walks away.

I stay quiet and continue with the tour while Hamisi explains the village life. The people in the village work hard. Some are blessed with maize farms, working long hours in the heat to plant, grow and harvest. Other villagers raise cattle, milk the cows early in the morning and deliver to the local towns, walking miles every day. Many of the young sons have moved to the city for jobs and send money to their parents. Girls too, Hamisi tells us. Many girls are beginning to move to the city these days.

We reach a small school under the *banda* built by the community in an open space near the end of the village. The teacher hired by the city council of education resides at the village and is paid for her services by the officials. Stationery is not provided to the school. Instead, the children use branches to write on the sandy ground for practice. Mostly it is a verbal education, much tougher to study this way, but nevertheless the children *do* get to study. They seem to be attentive and enthusiastic to learn. The teacher shows them the phonetic sounds—A, E, I, O, U—on the cracked chalkboard propped against a tree. I watch her.

"Okay, repeat after me: KALAMU, PENCIL," the teacher says.

"KALAMU," the children repeat. Then the next word is read. I think of Dada Zakiya and her teaching style, how we sat behind the car and read for hours, her long fingers moving over the letters. And god forbid, if I read phonetically, she would scold me. "This is English! Read properly." What a blessing she was. My Dada Zakiya, I call out to her in my thoughts. I miss her more than anyone can ever imagine, especially today. I wonder if she is feeling the same right now, at this very moment. I want to believe she is, but after what Hamisi told me about her, I am not sure.

Josephine and I walk back on the country road to town and our bus stop. I reflect on our two-day visit and how important it was for Hamisi to forgive me. My burden has lightened. Hamisi welcomed us to visit him again for a longer stay. I can still taste his spinach curry and beans, prepared with the Indian spices, and *ugali*. I take a moment to capture the country freshness and pleasure one last time, dropping a fistful of the soil into the *kikapu* as a souvenir for Emanuel. Josephine is bubbly and speaks of all the people and the village life. I grab her by the waist and squeeze her tight against me, seeing the sparks in her, just like the glittering stars. But I question myself: Why did she not have her nightmares at the village? Was it because she did not fear the pimp anymore, or was it because she was out of the prison, my home? I cannot help but wonder if she regrets the move and misses her pimp, her customers and her lifestyle of luxury.

~

The night sets and the bus lights dim. Josephine collapses against the window, exhausted from the long walk. I take her *kanga* pack and make a pillow out of it for the bumpy road. She settles on my shoulder instead. "I love you, Josephine," I say. She does not respond and I wonder if she heard me.

I think about Hamisi's comfortable retirement. He surely earned his dues by dedicating his long and honest service to Dada Zakiya's family. I, too, hope to retire with such privileges from Mrs. Scott. I imagine growing old with Josephine, the mother of my two children, who have had a chance to go to school. One of them is a *mwalimu*, teacher, and the other a *daktari,* doctor. I also dream that Dada Zakiya meets them and is very proud of me.

I feel restless when I think of what Hamisi told me about Dada Zakiya. "She would have left without saying goodbye to all of us anyway. Mama Fatima just took advantage of the unfortunate event of her watch getting stolen. Mama Fatima had already planned to trick her and send her away to her auntie so she could discreetly sell her house and business. She did not want Zakiya to know that she was planning to move all along."

When Mama Fatima left to join Dada Zakiya at her auntie's, Hamisi asked her if he could accompany her to say goodbye to Dada Zakiya, after which he would make his way to the village. Mama Fatima refused. She gave Hamisi many of her belongings and a bus ticket to the village. She paid him enough to finish building his house and buy chickens.

The sadness of not saying goodbye deepened when he spoke of Dada Zakiya. "I had promised her grandmother that I would take care of her," he cried. "Not even once did they come back to visit or bother to write a letter." What disturbed Hamisi the most was that Mama Fatima did not have the good intention of letting Dada Zakiya fulfill her dreams. She planned to get her married and settle her in a nice home with a good *Wahindi* foreigner. She did not want Dada Zakiya to have any more freedom.

Dada Zakiya always told me, "You have to believe in yourself, Juma, break the cycle. Yes, you can dream," and with that thought, I believe that Dada Zakiya will never allow Mama Fatima to stop her from achieving the dreams she is so passionate about. She was born to be a doctor, and I am sure she is going to be one. It may be one of the toughest fights she ever has with her mother, but somehow, definitely, she will win.

I close my eyes and silently pray for her.

The long bus ride comes to an end at half past seven in the morning of the next day. At least six buses, including ours, pull into the station, creating a yellow haze of dust. The screams and shouts of people at the bus depot make me want to turn back to the village. Aggressive taxi drivers grab people's bags, taking them forcefully, while tired

passengers tag along. *Whatever*, they are probably thinking, *just get us home.*

Josephine shakes her head. "Welcome to the real
world."

"The reality is that we walk," I say jokingly, despite the
headache I have, as if someone is hitting me with a cricket
bat. "Did you notice that no one grabbed our bags?"

"You mean the *kikapu*." She laughs so loud that people around us stare, wondering about our conversation,
maybe envious of our morning energy.

Halfway to town, we stop at the teashop *banda*. The
chai relieves my headache, but I am still worried about
giving the heartbreaking news to Maria tomorrow. She
will be devastated to find out that even Hamisi does not
have Dada Zakiya's address. Part of me wishes I had never
gone to see Hamisi. I had believed that Dada Zakiya and
her family cared for him and were in touch with him.
Then again, I should be happy about clearing my name
with Hamisi. He welcomed me as family, and I am
thankful.

As promised, Josephine and I roam the town, going
from shop to shop to find Ponds. She gets upset with a
shopkeeper who does not give her a straight answer, and
storms out of the shop. "You have to use a friendly style,"
I say. "You know they hide products behind the stores,
and that is why he is giving you strange answers. You act
like you have not grown up in this place and do not know
the ways." She raises her hands to the sky and walks a few

steps away from me. "How about I come back on Saturday and see if I have better luck," I say, grabbing her by
the waist. I tickle her to make her laugh.

"Hey, this is my trick," she says, frowning at me.

"Works on me. I always laugh when you tickle."

She nods and smiles but does not laugh. Gosh! She can
be stubborn at times. We head to the ferry berth. Sitting
on a log by the shore, we exchange good conversation
about village life, but it does not last for long. Eventually,
thoughts of the city, of city life, of city air hit Josephine
and she loses interest. "Do you believe he is not searching
for me anymore?" she whispers and looks down.

Instantly I feel drained. "He is not coming back.
Ever!" I scream. Once again, he is back in her thoughts
and it is the three of us in this relationship. Josephine
buries her face in her hands. I take a deep breath. I should
not have screamed at her. Besides, she is right. Is he really
gone? I feel a knot in my guts, as though someone is
squeezing my intestines, reminding me that he is still
present in our lives. I wrap my arm around her shoulder.
"He is not coming back." I say it softly this time. We
stare at the ocean for a long time.

foreigners
june 1985

FREEDOM KIOSK CLOSES at two in the afternoon on Saturdays, giving me plenty of time to shop before the ferry departure. Normally, my first stop is at the *sokoni* to find the good deals on vegetables and fruits. Today, for some reason, I feel a strong urge to pass by Darkhana first. When I get there, I feel Dada Zakiya's presence everywhere, as if she is calling me. I reflect on our happy times together, but when I think back, I realize how much I bothered her. "Find me work, Dada. You must," I would say, all the time. She would check my height and politely tell me to grow just a little taller first; then she would buy me my favourite fried chicken *figo*, chicken kidneys, with freshly squeezed lemon to make me feel better. We would sit on the Darkhana steps and talk about our future while I ate. Her smile was enough for me to survive one more day with hope and dreams. What Hamisi told me about Dada Zakiya still bothers me, so I have taken a vow to recite a prayer for her every night until the new moon, a prayer Dada Zakiya taught me. "It's our secret," she said. "Do not let anyone know of this. Recite it thirty-three times, and if you pray from your heart, God will hear you."

I walk to her flat and stand by the foot of the stairs. I expect magic—to see her run down the stairs and surprise me. I still imagine her being there. I close my eyes and hold onto the memories she left behind in the country where she was born and raised and shared her love. I do not want this moment of pleasure to end. The street speaks to me. It tells me that regardless of the changes in this city, my memories are my own, and that will never change.

This city street, once dominated by pioneer *Wahindi* merchants, has many new faces. While previous *Wahindi* shopkeepers have moved out of the country, to be replaced by others from small towns, many foreigners are venturing into new businesses—as long as they can tolerate the politics of *magendo*, bribe. The foreigners' advantage is the power of the dollar. They get permits easily, and sure enough, their new business idea is a success. Such is the *Chana Bateta and Bhajia* house next to Darkhana, now owned by a lady who returned from the other side of the ocean. She opened a pizza place, a new taste in town, and I hear she generates plenty of money. The place is always packed, and people say it is worth the wait and high price. Meantime, the owner keeps her "out of the country status," and one day she will return to her foreign land with all the money she has earned. Maria tells me there is more money in these new businesses than I could possibly count. And yet the city gets tougher each day for workers like me.

The movie theatres are not as packed as they used to be. I heard Maria's customer, who works at the film censor board, tell her that it is too expensive to get good movies, so only B-grade ones are shown. But lots of people own a television and VCR and do not want to go to the theatres when they can get together for a party and watch movies in the comfort of their home. *Wahindi* who have opened video-rental businesses from their homes make copies of Hindi movies, and in the first night they make back everything they paid for the original; the rest is all profit. When the street vendors at the beach by the theatres saw their business declining, they adapted by moving to the beach nearer to the Agakhan hospital, close to the residential area. They had to walk a long distance to this new spot, but that's the way it is. I've been there only once, shortly before Josephine moved in with me, in the hope of finding Samuel. But like Samuel said, "I am the best *mwizi*, thief, and you will never be able to catch up with me."

I remember how I used to walk frantically around the city, searching for Samuel at every possible corner. I stayed on the street on Friday nights, hoping he would come to the night ladies for his worldly pleasures. The toughest part was searching for him in the *sokoni* area, where we did our black market business. It reminded me of all my sins and lies, of my arrest and finally his revenge. Lately, my search for him has been casual, as though I have given up, or do not care. No, that is not true—I care. It's just that my time has been occupied with Josephine's demands and worries. My heart aches, and I decide to get serious about this again. I have often thought about visiting the Pombe House, though I doubt that Samuel would stoop so low as to use the cheap *malaya's* services. I am running out of options.

After purchasing vegetables and fruits, I go to the provision store to see if I'll have any luck finding Ponds. The cashier suggests I go to the chemist. The chemist suggests I go to the textile stores. I try another store and another and another. "Go see the herb doctor," one of the shopkeepers says. "He keeps things hidden. Maybe he can help." Although merchandise is becoming impossible to find—even simple things like talcum powder—I am optimistic and walk two streets to the herb doctor to find Ponds.

When I get there, a group of *Wahindi* ladies gathered by his closed shop are engaged in a serious conversation. I overhear one lady telling the others that his shop was searched and they found tubes of Colgate in his possession, so he has been arrested and taken to jail. His wife tried to pay for his release, but that is no longer easy.

I am shocked. Why jail? Police officials' finding illegal imported goods in the back storage of shops is not unusual. In fact, it is to their advantage. They get their share, the shopkeeper gets his share, and the consumer gets the product—everyone is happy. This is going to be a big mess, I think, as warrants have been issued for many shopkeepers. People are throwing away whatever may get them into trouble. Many did not get the message in time, and there are probably over a dozen in prison already.

"My son is here on holidays and has brought me Charlie perfume," says one of the ladies. "I better rush home, break the bottle and throw it out," and she runs home panic-stricken. The rest of them watch her go, laughing and gossiping about how she always overreacts.

I do not understand why shopkeepers need to be arrested. What is their crime? If there is anyone who needs to be arrested, it is the bloody pimp and that bastard Samuel. My thoughts race in rage, and I walk away, wondering how much *magendo* it will take to get all those shopkeepers out of jail. I bet it will be costly. Maybe things will cool off by next weekend. Until then Josephine will have to do without her beauty cream.

The residents look at each other and shrug when we get off the ferry. Two expensive boats are anchored by the shore, surrounded by officials and a group of foreigners having a discussion. When I get home, Josephine blurts out, "Did you see those people or were they gone?"

"What's going on?" I ask, but with the panic in her voice, I do not expect good news.

Indeed.

Later on that night, we have a community meeting, with everyone bringing their lanterns and taking a spot. "How are we going to fight this?" one of the elder men says.

"It is a way of life now," another resident screams in anger. "The rich get richer and the poor die." Many others scream and shout, to the point that no one is really listening. Esta, seated next to me, screams as well, but I do not hear her words. Josephine gets up and leaves. Emanuel looks confused and grips my hand for comfort. And here I am, in the middle of this chaos, quietly observing this madness. I clap my hands to draw attention. "Quiet! Quiet!" I raise my voice and continue clapping until there is silence.

"It is understandable that the country needs money," I say, "and the classy resort built by foreigners on this land will attract tourists and create a lot more jobs. But what about us? We will be displaced. So let us discuss this calmly and come up with a solution."

Everyone is sad, angry and frustrated all at the same time, but they listen. I tell them about the warrants and the shopkeepers being arrested today. They worry more about the corruption and inflation. Once again, we will see the same pattern—shopkeepers moving out of the country and foreigners moving in, taking the best business opportunities and then sending their money back to their own countries. Meantime, we continue struggling, hoping only to feed ourselves at least one meal a day.

After nearly an hour, we agree to form a petition and take it to the officials to stop the foreigners from buying our land, our homes.

displaced
june 1985

"THERE IS NO way in hell I am going to be homeless," I shout at the stars, even though I know that no one gives a shit. I point at the brightest one, threatening. "Are you listening?" But the bloody star continues to glitter. I complain further, this time about Josephine, who has deserted me and gone to sleep. She refuses to talk to me, as if it is my fault that the officials are giving our land away. Esta appears, putting her hand on my shoulder and staring at me with bloodshot eyes. "It's late, go to sleep. We'll work this out together," she says, and runs back to her hut before I say anything.

I speak to Mrs. Scott the next day about the foreigners invading my livelihood. "I am sure the government will move you elsewhere," she says. "There is plenty of space further out in the rural areas. They surely cannot just kick you out." She speaks casually, not fully understanding the impact on my neighbourhood family.

"That's bullshit," Maria says, not caring if Mrs. Scott is offended. "Since when has this government cared about the poor? The officials take bribes and only look after their own interests. You don't expect the fishermen to walk from the rural areas with their dhows every morning, do you?" Maria pauses and looks at me. "What if we find a way to move you into National Housing?"

National Housing is a government-subsidized, one-bedroom, cement flat with kitchen and sitting room. It also provides electricity and water—when available. With my low income, I would qualify, but I would need influence to get on the housing list. Maria tells me that her nephew Abbasi has connections and might be able to assist. Then she explains to Mrs. Scott that my case would be stronger with her help.

"What can I do?" Mrs. Scott asks with enthusiasm.

"If you accompany Abbasi to the application office, and with you being *Muzungu*, Juma's chances are higher," Maria says.

"Absolutely, as long as your nephew is organized and knows what he is doing," Mrs. Scott says.

Maria nods. "I will talk to him tonight."

But there are two problems with this plan. First, to qualify, I need to have a family, so I decide to adopt Esta and Emanuel and share the housing with them. Besides, I cannot allow them to be displaced, and I am certain they will be happy sharing with me. The second problem, the one that worries me more, is the cost of the bribe for the application. I hope Mrs. Scott will lend me the money, considering the situation.

I talk to Esta about the National Housing plan, and she bursts into tears of joy, as if a burden has been lifted off her shoulders. "It will be easy to pretend to be your mother," she says, and for the first time she gives me a motherly hug. "We can split the rooms into two."

"Yes, there will be a sitting room too. Maybe that can be converted into a sleeping area for you and Emanuel," I say.

"Please, God." Her face sags. "I pray we get the house."

"Have faith," I say.

We decide not to discuss this matter with either Josephine or Emanuel for now, as they tend to talk too much. We need to keep quiet so no one gets the same idea.

A week later, at the next community meeting, we are told that the petition to stop the development has been rejected. We must start making alternate arrangements so that when the time comes we have a place to go. There is no mention of moving us to any other area, as Mrs. Scott had thought. The officials say that the investors are still in the process of planning, and it will take four or five months, which buys us time. In the meantime, we submit a new petition for compensation for our loss so we can afford to build a new hut if we find a space elsewhere.

"What are we going to do, where will we go, huh!" Josephine raises her voice. "People are talking about the slums. Don't expect me to live there."

"Mrs. Scott will help us, I have talked to her. Unless you have a better plan." I am so disturbed by her rudeness that I raise my voice as well.

"I said I am not moving to the slums with you," and once again she stomps out of the meeting and goes home alone.

"See, this is why I prefer not to tell her anything," I complain to Esta. "She is unreasonable and doesn't think before she speaks. If only once she were supportive, only once." Esta stays out of it and keeps quiet on the walk home.

Abbasi keeps active, checking the progress of the National Housing and reporting it to Mrs. Scott. She was good enough to give the filing clerk two hundred shillings to start the process and make it happen. Maria assures us that Abbasi is an honest man who keeps his word, and I believe her. My intuition about him was good the minute he shook my hand. He does not need to do this for me, at least not for free, and yet he does. He visits us twice a week to let us know that he is still working with the clerks.

Three months pass and Abbasi comes by just before closing. "I have great news. You are on the top of the list," he says. "There is an elderly couple retiring and going back to their village soon. Their son is getting married and moving to a different town with his wife. Once their flat is vacant, it is yours."

I exhale and drop to the floor, rubbing my head. "Thank you, God," I say. Both Maria and Mrs. Scott watch me with a warm smile. Mrs. Scott hands Abbasi the additional two hundred shillings she had promised to pay the filing clerk once my application was ready for processing. "*Ahsante sana*, Mrs. Scott. I will pay you back."

She laughs, knowing that I will not pay her back, but my heart wants to think so and maybe she does too. "Well, this better work, or else, Maria, your nephew is going to have a lot to answer for," she says, looking right into Abbasi's eyes.

"It will work, Mrs. Scott. I am confident," Abbasi says.

"Come by tomorrow after work and I will treat you to a beer," I tell Abbasi before heading home.

In the meantime, closer to the shore, the officials and foreigners are taking pictures, sketching plans and tying yellow ribbons to the coconut trees. They are here. As we step out of the ferry, I see the disappointment and sadness on the faces of every passenger. No one talks. We pass the unwelcome intruders quietly, with our heads hung low. Halfway overland, I stop by a tree and give it a hug. The man behind me seems to understand. Others follow suit and hug the trees too. Then we walk home in despair.

Once again we gather for a community meeting to

receive the disappointing news that our petition has been rejected. We are not going to be compensated, and it is our responsibility to find new homes. Josephine screams as usual, creating a big scene. The neighbours ignore her as if her views, complaints and suggestions are not important. As much as I am tempted to tell her about the National Housing to quiet her down, I remain silent. Yes, it may not be fair, but I cannot take chances with her loud mouth.

"You promised me freedom," she cries like a child once we reach home.

"This is not a time to fight, Josephine." I do not bother to soothe her tears. "This is when we need each other's strength."

"What about the devil?" she asks. She stomps into the room and drops onto the mattress, covering her face with the pillow. I leave her alone. No more, I think to myself. She must deal with her demons herself. I cannot expend all my energy on her; there is too much to do.

At least I have good news for Esta. We both pray that the elderly couple vacates the National Housing before we are kicked out of our homes. I notice how much she has aged recently. She asks me if she will truly be allowed to live in the housing with me. I assure her that I will not abandon her. "Your name is there on the application form as my mother. No matter what, the house is yours as well," I say.

"What name have you given?" she asks.

"The Kipanga family."

"Kipanga, a falcon. Is that what your name is?"

"Yes, J.K. are my initials. I am Juma Kipanga. And from here on, you are Esta Kipanga, with my brother Emanuel Kipanga, and Mrs. Josephine Kipanga is my wife. We stick to this and we are a family, allowed to stay together in the National Housing."

"Well, then, Kipanga it is." She smiles and pats my shoulder.

The next day, Abbasi and I go to the bar after work. I buy us a cold bottle of Tusker, and he gives me more news about the elderly couple. "The wedding is planned during Christmas. Another three months to go."

"Are they moving out right after the wedding?" I ask. Abbasi does not know the details. We both assume that the parents will take another two or three months to move out after their son's wedding. "All right then, about six months at least." I rub my forehead.

"Sorry. I cannot make it faster," he says.

"Oh no, you have done more than you will ever know. Thank you, man." I offer him another bottle.

He looks at his watch. "Won't you miss your ferry?" he asks.

"I am not going home tonight," I say. I gesture to the bartender to give us each another bottle, even though I cannot afford it; the free bowl of roasted peanuts with each drink makes up for it. I tell Abbasi all about Samuel. I cannot allow anything to distract me from my plan to search for him, and tonight I intend to go to the cheap prostitutes' section of town. I have a strong feeling about this.

"I will come with you," he says. "Later on you can come to my place for the night. Just buy me fish and chips for dinner, and don't tell Maria."

"I will not tell," I say. However, I do not have enough cash left for fish and chips, so instead we order a side plate of salty fried *dagaa*, sardines, at the bar and share it before heading out into the rough streets to look for Samuel.

pombe house
september 1985

ABBASI AND I enter the smoked-filled Pombe House. The distinctive *bhangi,* marijuana, smoke burns my eyes and I struggle to see. "What is this shit?" Abbasi says, clearing his throat. I check around for Samuel, squinting for a better look, but deep inside I know he will not be here. Samuel has better taste than to come to this third-class dump. Abbasi steps on a broken beer bottle on the filthy floor. A small piece of glass snaps and flies over his foot, and he almost trips on a woman. "Shit, man," he says.

"I think we've made a mistake. Let's get out of here," I say, looking around one more time before leaving the bar, disappointed.

With a handkerchief over his nose, Abbasi bolts for the door. "I almost fainted in there," he says. "I never thought I'd appreciate the outside air so much."

We pass by the cheap *malaya*, hookers, in their house of pleasures, with no doors, only curtains drawn around the beds. In one, with the curtain not fully drawn, a big man lies atop a *malaya*, groaning, his body racing non-stop while the *malaya* chews gum and checks her nails. Abbasi finds it entertaining and stands by the front veranda laughing. One of the *malaya* approaches him. "I can give you two for one," she says, smacking her lips. She's an ugly woman—red shiny dress, bright red lipstick, no class. Maria would be disgusted with her hairstyle.

"Okay, time to get out of here before any of these diseased women touches me," Abbasi says. I can see that he is starting to freak out.

In the corner, a man struggles to negotiate with one of the hookers. She finally agrees and takes him behind the fence for a quick job standing up. The cheap bastard pays her less than they agreed. She grabs the money, swears and spits on him. We rush out of sight and into the alley. As we walk out of the area, an expensive Pajero drives by, occupied by three *Wahindi* boys. The driver slows down and lowers the window. "Hey, do you have any *bhangi?*" he asks.

"We are customers. Check further inside," Abbasi says, motioning behind us. "Be careful, it is not safe here."

"Let's get out of here," the passenger in the back says. "I told you boys this is a bad idea."

"Oh *shetap*, shut up!" the boy in the front shouts. They drive towards the Pombe House.

"Want to bet they are dead meat?" I say.

Abbasi claps my hand. "And if not, the *bhangi* will destroy them eventually."

With only the moonlight for visibility, we walk the dark dirt road, making our way back to the main street, hoping to reach safety. Drunkards stagger by, some falling into the ditch at the side of the road. They swear or take a piss, oblivious of their surroundings. Ahead, we hear the high-pitched scream of a woman in the ditch. I feel ashamed to have brought Abbasi to such a dangerous place and involved him in my problems. I must get him home safe. But it seems Abbasi has no fear. He moves towards the scream. "We must help her."

I grab hold of him. "Leave it alone! It will only get us in trouble. This is not how it's supposed to end."

"Not with the two of us," he says and jumps into the ditch. I follow him. "Shit, she's a girl, a young girl. You shit." He punches the man. The man punches him back and slaps the girl. I quickly grab hold of the man. He fights to hold onto the girl, but she tears at his face, scrambles up the ditch and runs. "Hey! Wait," Abbasi says, and goes after her.

"What the fuck," the man yells. "Come back, you bitch." He tries to follow her. His voice takes me by surprise. I grab his foot and pull him back in. "Fuck, fuck," he yells again, fighting back.

I drop him flat on his back, and just then, in the moonlight, I see the devil's face. My body turns cold. But then I feel Josephine touching and warming me up. "Finish him," she says. "You promised, remember?" Without a moment's hesitation, I sit on the devil's chest, pull my knife from my pocket and slit his face. My heart races with fear, rage and pleasure—all at the same time. The devil presses his palms over his face and screams. His screech of agony excites me. I think of young Josephine, the first time I saw her with the devil, and how he slapped her face. I feel angry for not having been able to stop him then. I am fed up with him coming between Josephine and me. Even in his absence, he is present all the time.

He fights to free himself, breathing heavily, smelling drunk. "Let me go, you fuck, let me go," he shouts, kicking his legs in the air, making it difficult for me to hold him down.

"Don't let him free!" I hear Josephine's voice in my head. I struggle to keep him steady. He manages to raise his head and knocks my face with it. His hands now free on my chest, he pushes me. He gains energy and gets stronger, and I must not allow it. I cover his face with my palm and push until his head touches the ground. I quickly hold the knife to his throat, just as I did before, except this time I am not bluffing. He suddenly surrenders, which scares me because it feels like he is tricking me. "Kill him, Juma. What are you waiting for?" Josephine wants him dead. I make sure to keep the knife steady and close to his throat. My hand trembles and my heart continues to race. Sweat burns my eyes.

"Give me one good reason why I shouldn't kill you?" I say, blinking. The moonlight shines on his bloody face and his eyes plead for mercy. My heart returns to normal as I take control. "I want you to look at that cut on your face every morning and remind yourself that I am watching you," I say and dig deeper with my knife. With blood running down his neck, reaching the ground, he screams louder, but no one cares. I put my mouth to his ear and he goes silent. "If I hear one more word on the street that you are searching for Josephine, I will kill you." He lies there, no struggle, no word, no scream. I see *young* Josephine, laughing and running free on the street, hugging every night lady, telling them about my bravery in rescuing her. Yes, this is the way it is supposed to end.

I jump out of the ditch and go searching for Abbasi. He is at the far end of the street, running towards me and calling. "Are you okay? I am sorry, but that girl . . ." I don't let him finish the sentence. Together we run.

Abbasi lends me his shirt. After a quick wash, we sit on his sofa and sip the fresh *kahawa*, espresso, he has prepared.

"What was all that blood on your shirt. What happened?" Abbasi asks. "He could have killed you. I should have listened to you in the first place."

"You did the right thing," I say. "The man in the ditch was coming after you both." I pat his shoulder. "You are a good man, Abbasi." Then I ask, "Do you believe in karma?"

"I call it luck," Abbasi says, and pours more *kahawa* from an Arabic carafe made of copper. "Many things could have gone wrong tonight."

"No! We were meant to be there and save that girl."

"What was that stupid girl doing with him at that time of night anyway?" he asks.

I shrug. Little does he know that she could have been another Josephine, sold by her mother, forced to be with him. "Karma. We were meant to save her, and that's all we need to believe."

The next morning, I head out early. "What's the rush," Abbasi asks.

"I need to go for a walk," I say. "Thanks for helping last night."

"Better luck next time, *rafiki*, friend. Or better yet, it's not worth it. Forget about Samuel."

"I think you're right. I will forget about him," I say, and decide to keep Abbasi out of Samuel and my affair.

I take long strides down the streets towards the beach and run along the shore for over an hour. The morning sun is already hot and I am drenched in sweat. I head to the ferry berth and walk along the barge towards the anchored ferry. I take the knife out of my pocket. Its work is done—I do not need it anymore—and I drop it under the barge into the ocean. I am as fearless as a lion. The devil dares not come to my territory. I pass by the church and stand there for a moment and pray before starting a fresh, beautiful day.

The police have blocked the street and no one is allowed to enter the shops. Maria stands with the crowd. She calls out to me and I push through the crowd to get to her. "What's going on?" I ask.

"Apparently, the maid is devastated by whatever she saw in one of the motel rooms. There she is, being interrogated by the police." Maria points. "Mrs. Scott left for home. She has asked us to take the day off. 'This will be a long day,' she told me. 'You know how disorganized the police are. We may as well go home.' I was waiting for you to arrive. I guess we can go now."

"You go on," I say and wait around for the scoop.

More than two hours pass. Sushmita is upset. "So many sick patients are waiting to see the doctor. They should at least let *us* carry on with our work." Finally, we see police workers carrying two stretchers with covered bodies out of the motel room. Someone has died. In a short while, the street opens up. The restaurant and butcher resume business, and patients settle in the dispensary to wait for the doctor. The garage remains closed for the day.

The motel manager gives us the news. "It was one of the night girls, Sophie. She killed her pimp and herself. I am told they arrived from out of town yesterday and had a fight." This cannot be happening. The blood rushes to my heart. I can hear it pounding and hold tight to my chest while I listen to the manager pass on the police report.

The maid found the pimp's dead body in the bathtub. The investigators think that there must have been a fight and Sophie cut his face badly. He must have been weak from such a deep cut and got into the bathtub to wash or recover. Or maybe he passed out. Sophie took advantage and cut both his wrists. Then she hung herself with a bedsheet tied to the ceiling fan. The police say it is clearly a murder suicide.

"Nothing makes sense," one of the night ladies says. "Last night, the pimp beat Sophie with a leather belt, and he was shouting at her, telling her she was ugly and a liability because no one got pleasure from her."

"I know, I heard it too," another night lady says. "He was screaming and telling her that he was going to purchase a much prettier girl. He left Sophie in the room beaten up. He was too strong for her to cut his face."

"I saw him all bloodied up with a cut face, staggering up the stairs," another one says. "Then he shouted *no* when he walked into the room. I think Sophie had already hung herself. So how could she have murdered him?"

The manager puts a stop to the night ladies. "I suggest you all shut up. What difference does it make who killed whom? It's not worth the police's time. They gain nothing from a dead-end case." He gestures to the ladies to leave. "As far as I am concerned, good riddance to the dead ones. They were nothing but trouble on my street. Now, move on, everyone. Let's get on with our lives."

Case closed.

Josephine dances in circles. I have not seen her so happy since our return from the village. She pulls me out of the hut and we run towards the ocean. A full moon shines on her face. She walks along the shore, splashing water with her feet, dancing and singing. This is the Josephine I fell in love with. "He is dead, that bastard is dead," she rejoices. "I can roam free in this world. I can do whatever I want. I can be a star." She reaches out to me and kisses me passionately. We find a perfect spot, listen to the ocean and make love.

I have only told her my version of the pimp's death, that he was murdered by some thugs and dumped in a ditch. She does not need to know about Sophie. Her death may raise disturbing questions. The fact that the devil is in hell is all that matters, and that is all she needs to know.

Holding hands, we walk back to the hut to start a happy life.

slums
october 1985

TWO MONTHS' NOTICE has been handed to us to vacate our homes. The bulldozers are moving further and further in, stripping the land, and by early next year the construction will have reached the huts. I had not realized how big this area was without the countless trees and bushes. Most of the residents have already moved out. Some have joined their extended families in rural areas, probably cramped together in small spaces. The majority of them have moved to the slums. A few of us are still around, buying time despite knowing it is hopeless.

Abbasi is apologetic when he tells me that the retiring parents may extend their stay at the National Housing flat a little longer. The wife needs an operation for cataracts and her doctors have told her to wait a while. That means we wait, too. In the meantime, Josephine pressures me. I decide to tell her the full plan. "I have good news, big, surprising news." I hold her hand and she smiles. I tell her about the National Housing, and how Maria's nephew Abbasi is helping with the process and Mrs. Scott is paying the bribes. I tell her that our application has been accepted but that we should keep quiet until we have our new home. She jumps up off her stool and knocks me to the ground as if she is attacking me like a dog. I bump my head and we laugh and laugh and laugh. Pleasure echoes throughout our hut.

"God loves us. Two pieces of good news in a month. We will have a wonderful life. I can see a bright light ahead. Imagine us living in the city, not worrying about that bloody devil . . ."

I interrupt. "Please, Josephine, please. There is not going to be another mention of that bastard again. He is dead, and I want him out of our life, forever."

"Okay, okay," she says. "I can have a kitchen, walk to the market . . ." I give her a hug while she talks and dreams.

"Esta and Emanuel will be sharing the house with us," I say. She pushes me. I explain the situation and tell her that, anyway, we could not abandon them. "We will have our own private life, but this is the way it is. Besides, they are family. What is your problem?" She squints and presses her lips together. I remind her how kind Esta was to her, getting her started in the business. It was Esta who advised me to take her on a vacation. I also remind her how she wished she had a mother like Esta. But Josephine forgets, because she is selfish. She wants everything for herself. As I think about it, I realize that it has always been this way. How childish she gets when I do not meet her demands. *I need Ponds, I need a new kanga, I need scented soap*—a never-ending *I need*. And last week, when I mentioned that Mr. Scott had agreed to see her about a job at the shrimp processing plant, she got angry with me. "Eew!" she whined. "I will smell like a fisherman. No matter how many times they wash up, they still smell of fish." The conversation turned into a quarrel, and in the end I gave up. She won, but lost the job opportunity. This time she can sulk all she wants. Esta and Emanuel are moving with us—and that is final.

A month later, together with Esta and Emanuel, Josephine and I visit the slums. I know what to expect; this is not my first visit. Everywhere there is trash, feces, skinny stray dogs and cats. Josephine is shocked. She stops abruptly and throws up. "No! No!" she says and runs out of the area.

Esta blinks and clings to Emanuel, reassuring him that this is a short passage in life and they can pull through it together. We notice a group of children Emanuel's age sniffing glue. Their ribs pop out and their stomachs bulge. Emanuel runs towards another group of boys playing football. Esta begins to cry. "This is a rough place.

He should not be playing with those boys."

"We will keep him safe," I say. "Besides, we have jobs. We will not allow him to get to that state. Now do you understand why educating him is so important?" We walk the entire place to get a better idea of the space available, what to bring with us and how to build our temporary home with corrugated tin.

In the evening when we are home, Esta talks to Josephine. "My dear, this is only for a short while. Look how far Juma has come, from a beggar to a decent job and a wonderful wife to come home to. He provides you with food and love. This is a time when he needs your support."

"I am not his wife," Josephine snaps. Then she turns to me. "This is not what I signed up for," and she runs off.

I decide not to go after her. She will only create a scene and embarrass me, which has happened more than once. I tell Esta not to bother trying to mend our relationship. But it gets dark and late, and Josephine does not return. For almost two hours, Emanuel and I search every possible spot. Finally, I take him back to the hut. Esta is worried. "Go check the shore," she says.

"We did," Emanuel says and crashes in his sleeping area.

I fill up the lantern with kerosene and head out to search for her again. It should not be so difficult. Why can I not find her? I should have run after her; it was

unkind of me to let her go when she was hurting. Around
ten o'clock, while I am still searching, I hear her voice at
Kitema's hut. Kitema is a neighbour whom Josephine
speaks highly of. "Why don't you find a job like his?"
Josephine often asks me. "Kitema gets to bring leftover
food from the household where he works, and the owners
have bought him a bicycle. They are nice to him and have
agreed to let him sleep on their terrace until he finds a
decent place to move to, not the slums."

I place the lantern by Kitema's doorstep and walk in.
Josephine stands topless in front of Kitema, who pushes
her away. "What's going on?" I ask.

Josephine hangs on tight to Kitema, but he continues
to push her. "Go back, Josephine," he says. "Take her
away, she is so forceful." He seems to be pleading with me
to rescue him. I slap her. "How could you?" Then I grab
her and drag her all the way to our place.

Esta rushes out of her hut and stands with her hand on
her mouth, watching Josephine scream. "Juma!" Esta says,
trying to stop me.

"Don't interfere, Esta. This is none of your business." I
drag Josephine into the hut and grab my belt. "You *malaya*!
You *malaya*! You *malaya*!" I shout with every whip, until
Esta barges in and gets in the way. "Leave and never come
back. I have freed you from the devil. Now go!" Josephine
lies helpless on the floor, bleeding. Esta kneels down and
pulls her close, hugging and rocking her. I take off towards
the beach and sleep there for the night.

three

national housing
august 1986

WE MOVE INTO the National Housing flat. Mr. and Mrs.
Scott attend our party, bringing lavish food and a book
set for Emanuel. Neighbours with their children join us.
Maria and Abbasi are our guests of honour; we toast and
wish them the best in life. I think of Josephine and picture her being with us. She is wearing a blue dress, the
colour I loved best on her. Her hair has been finely braided
in the latest style by Mama Kiosk. She is offering bottles of
Coca-Cola to the guests. Why did things have to happen
the way they did? The question saddens me.

I try not to think of the night at Kitema's, her pleading
with another man to look after her. It felt as if someone
had stabbed an arrow into my heart. She hung on tight to
his arm, not letting go even when he pushed her away.
The next day was the worst; she didn't utter a word. On

the ferry, she stood at the far end and even refused to speak to Esta. That evening when she did not return to the ferry, I knew I had lost her forever.

"She was scared to live in the slums," Esta told me when we moved into this new home. "You should go look for her and bring her home."

"She broke my trust. I can't."

"You're being stubborn," she said. "Kitema explained that she was flirting with him so he would take her to sleep on his employer's terrace. Nothing happened between them."

"She broke my trust," I say again.

Dada Zakiya used to tell me that true friends remain faithful in all circumstances. Josephine broke that trust and broke my heart. Now I need to move on without her. Still, I do appreciate the joy of my time with her and the comfort we gave each other when I lived on the street and she lived with the pimp. I cared, she cared—I am certain she cared then. I pray to God that she has learned the value of life and cherishes it. She is free. How she chooses to use her freedom is entirely up to her.

I go to the balcony for some fresh air. However narrow the space, it feels like heaven out here. I look at the shared water tap on the veranda downstairs and smile. I am amazed that I can carry buckets of water to our house at any time.

The sky is a deep purple, with endless stars. I smile at my lucky star and it twinkles back at me, but deep inside, my heart fills with sorrow. Once again, I am a lonely man.

The laughter continues in the party room. I cannot believe I lived in the slums for nine months. We almost lost Emanuel when he was attacked by a gang of boys who teased him out of jealousy for wearing a school uniform. God was watching over him that day and he was saved. Then there were the drunkards who took advantage of the women who live alone in the slums. Esta and Emanuel clung to me at night as though I were their guardian angel, while I lived in pain and fear. I worried that this might be a lifetime move for us. I needed Josephine at my side, assuring me that this, too, would pass and we would be okay.

The lights go off. Once again, the city is out of electricity. Esta and I turn on the lantern and light a few candles. Everyone at the party cheers.

independence day
december 1986

PREPARATIONS FOR A HUGE fair at the stadium to celebrate the twenty-fifth anniversary of Independence Day
excite the city. For the past three days, Mama Kiosk has
been braiding hair non-stop, through the lunch hour and
over two hours longer in the evening. Mrs. Scott has paid
me extra to wait around so I can take her safely to the car
at the end of the day. Since last week, diplomats and VIP
guests have been arriving, and the airport has been busy
with added security, meaning passengers are paying more
bribes to get through smoothly. One of the tourists, while
having her hair braided, asked Mrs. Scott if she could
help her find a room at the beach resort away from the
crowded city hotels. She wanted to relax and enjoy the
serenity of the beach. Mrs. Scott made a few phone calls
to the luxurious resorts over twenty miles away but had

no luck. Finally, she managed to find a perfect room at the new resort, which has been a number-one attraction since its opening.

I still remember the opening day of the resort, when Abbasi and I took the luxurious water taxi across. Esta refused to attend and did not allow Emanuel either. The resort looked like a magical kingdom, except that it was not my magical kingdom anymore. One could not imagine that over a year ago, this kingdom was my home and I had a little hut here, planning my life dreams. I once brought the love of my life to my proud home, to make her my life partner, wishing to have children with her one day. Together with my kingdom, I lost my queen forever.

The fairgrounds open at nine this morning. Esta and Emanuel, with other families in the building, wait for a *matatu* to get to the stadium. Because there is no guarantee how long the bus will be, and I have no patience to wait, I walk for almost two hours. Emanuel seemed disappointed but I promised to meet him there.

Five Shillings, the sign above the stadium gates reads. The crowd gathers by the entrance like a colony of ants. The two guards are unable to control them while the attendant collects the fees, so they block the entrance and scream at the crowd to form an orderly queue. In the meantime, two tour buses arrive. The drivers have a long discussion with the guards and hand out prepaid passes to the tourists, who go right through the gates and into the fair. The guards try to count heads, but there is a commotion as the locals become impatient. The guards are distracted, and I take advantage of the chaos and sneak in, in between a tourist couple, free of charge. The tourists smile at me and take my photo. I will probably make for a fun story when they get home, and I laugh out loud.

The sound of beautiful African drums pulls me towards the dancers, dressed in green, yellow and black patterned *kanga*. Young women dance in circles singing *sindhima, dhim, dhim, dhim, dhim*, moving one step forward on *sindhima*, and then swinging their buttocks side to side on *dhim, dhim, dhim, dhim*. What wonderful entertainment. I laugh and clap to this joyful celebration, thinking of Dada Zakiya and wishing she were here with me. She would have enjoyed the dancing and singing. Yes, the singing. How I long to hear her sing. I think of the drive-in cinema entertainment, almost seven years ago, and how she shocked us with her amazing voice. It still feels like yesterday.

I walk around, hoping to find Esta and Emanuel. I cannot wait to tell them how I got in free. I plan to take Emanuel to the squeaky merry-go-round later on. Maybe they are by the vendors, socializing with their friends. I get to the other side of the fence, where the barbeque smoke and aroma of *nyama choma choma* clearly guide me to the vendors, but I still do not see any sign of Esta and Emanuel.

I walk back around the fence. Four white Volvos drive

into the stadium to the foot of the stage. The officials, diplomats and VIP guests have arrived. The crowd claps and cheers and the band march begins. A proud drummer in front leads the marching children—from a prestigious school, I bet—to the stage. The *bendera*, flag, rises high, and with attention the crowd sings the national anthem with the marching band. I stand still and pay my respects, but I cannot help thinking of all the beggars on the street and the homeless children, like I once was, starving, and the slums, which continue to grow larger every day. Not everyone is privileged to meet Dada Zakiya and get a chance in life. Where did this nation go wrong? Why are there such vast differences? Rich and poor? Why is Mr. Scott able to take a net and catch shrimp and have such a lavish life while the fishermen in their small dhows struggle to live in their tiny homes? Why was Dada Zakiya living in such a comfortable flat and I on the street?

"*Uhuru! Uhuru*! Freedom! Freedom!" the crowd screams.

I browse at the stalls. People are selling *kanga*, bead necklaces, Makonde carvings, miniature zebra-skin drums, elephant-hair bangles, and so much more. There are lots of local *Wahindi* and many *Wazungu* tourists in the crowd. The stall keepers take advantage of the tourists, charging them triple the price. Ivory bangles are the most popular thing to buy. *Wahindi* know better; they do not purchase anything. They can drive to the local areas anytime and buy whatever they want at a bargain.

I speak to one of the stall keepers and admire his beautiful collection of beads. They would be perfect for Maria's braiding. He tells me he owns the largest *duka ya shanga*, bead shop, in the area, and I get directions to his store. I pick five of my favourite beads and purchase them at one shilling for Mrs. Scott. She will be happy, and maybe later she can visit the store and add to her collection.

My attention is drawn to a suspicious man at the *kikapu* stall by the fence. He is hanging near a woman who is browsing over the *vikapu*, baskets. Shit! I think in disbelief. Bloody hell, yes, it is Samuel. So this is where he has been, by the airport, probably robbing people, which seems to be his plan at this very moment. I sneak behind the fence, like a lion stalking its prey. To be absolutely sure, I peak at him again. He looks thin, but it is definitely him, with that ugly nose and scarred face. Unaware of what is going on, the woman reaches up to get a *kikapu* hanging over her head. Samuel waits for the right moment, and I know he always has an escape plan. Indeed, this is perfect, a perfect spot by the corner next to the fence, an easy run to the other side to blend in with the crowd. Except that I know his plan and I am standing right behind the fence, waiting for him.

He grabs the woman's purse and runs. The woman is frantic—she screams her lungs out—but he is too fast for her and has already turned to escape. I come out from behind the fence and stand right in front of him. He freezes, not expecting me, not expecting anyone to be guarding his escape.

"*Mwizi! Mwizi!*" I shout.

The woman screams again and people rush from every direction. He pushes me to the ground and sprints, but the vendors on the other side have already crowded him. Samuel is trapped.

"*Mwizi! Mwizi!*" louder voices echo from the crowd. The *mwizi* has been spotted from every side. One man jumps him and throws him to the ground. The woman's purse lands far away and she runs to grab it. Another man punches Samuel when he struggles to get up. People join in, and together they kick him. They kick him in the back, the stomach, the head. Samuel screams, shouts and cries, but no one can hear him. The crowd shouts. The woman shouts louder. "Finish the bastard." I stand there watching my helpless friend.

"Enough!" yells an old man from the crowd. "Let it go. He is dead." There is silence. Samuel's skull has been split. Blood oozes from his head, and I feel sick to my stomach. "Chh! Chh! Chh!" People click their tongues and shake their heads. "What a waste," someone says.

I approach the body and kneel next to him. "What are you doing?" I hear a voice from the crowd.

"Just checking if he is truly dead," I say and cover Samuel with my entire body. I put my ear to his chest, pretending to check his heartbeat.

"He is dead, all right," the woman says. "Get away

from him or you'll put yourself in trouble if the police arrive."

I sneak my hands into Samuel's pockets and grab whatever I can. I close my fists and put both hands on my waist as I get up. I nod. "Yes! He is dead. What a waste," and I walk away with the rest of the crowd. I empty my fists into my pockets, and then I run, run out of the fair, and run and run. I remove my bloody shirt and throw it away. With only my undershirt on, I take a taxi to the market and walk the rest of the way home.

The house is quiet. I remove my clothes and prance around. I drop to the ground. There is a knot in my stomach and my gut screams in pain. I warm some water on the stove and take it to the bathroom, where I wash my face and body, watching my dirt swirl down the drain as I pour the water over my head. I lie naked on the cement floor of my bedroom and stare at the trousers. I finally pick them up and empty the pockets. There are the beads I purchased and barely any money after the taxi. Samuel's Swiss knife—I remember the day he stole it and was so proud of himself. A piece of paper and something bundled in a handkerchief. I untie the knot and there it is: Dada Zakiya's watch. "Oh sweet god." I look up, rub my hands on my head, and I smile and sigh.

I take a good look at the watch. The hands have stopped at around a quarter past three. No problem, I think to myself. I can set the time and wind it when I give it back to Dada Zakiya. I take a fresh cloth, wipe the watch and store it in an empty coffee tin. I slit the foam under my mattress and stuff the tin into it. I borrow a roll of masking tape from Emanuel's stationery pile and secure the slit. No one will know.

But I cannot get Samuel's blood out of my mind. I breathe heavily and my body shakes. I feel like rot. I rush to the toilet and almost slip when I squat. Maybe that is where I belong, right down in the gutter, in the shit hole. My face feels sweaty. I must calm down before Esta and Emanuel arrive. I check myself in the cracked pocket mirror; the line splits my reflection into two. One side of my face is bright and happy: I have finally found Dada Zakiya's watch. The other side is pale: I see Samuel's brain split out of his head, his life ending painfully, and the joy I get out of it.

Forgive me, God, forgive me, I wail like a child.

kipanga
april 1987

MY MIND IS occupied with one thought and one thought only: *I must deliver the watch to its destiny.* The urge to free myself from this burden deepens, and each moment brings more anxiety and sorrow, till my very soul feels pain. My nights are sleepless and my rapid heartbeat scares me. When I ask Sushmita, she tells me that I must rest my mind and sleep. This time she refuses to give me medicine and instead brings me *tulsi*, holy basil. At night, I sip *tulsi* tea and try hard not to let my mind wander, but Samuel's last moments continue to haunt me.

I try to think of Dada Zakiya and our fond times together, letting these thoughts soothe me like a lullaby so that I can put myself to sleep. But Dada Zakiya is angry; she does not support me, and I hear her voice: "What have you done, good lord, what have you done?" I cover my ears with my palms to shut off the voices in my head.

Eventually, I fall asleep and Josephine visits my dreams. She curses me. I remind her that I am the good one. I am the one who freed her from the pimp. But she curses me still, for making her homeless, for not fulfilling the promises I made to her. She says she was better off with the pimp.

Once again, I wake up and go sleepless. Samuel visits me and laughs; I see his shadow pass by me. He corners me in a dark space, which never gets any lighter. Why? Why do I not see the brightness anywhere? Dada Zakiya used to make me believe that hopelessness had a lot of brightness hidden in it, because, with hopelessness, one creates hope and eventually sees the light. But me, I am going deeper into the hole, seeing darker than dark. There is no one to catch me as I fall. None of the people who mattered to me in my life are around me anymore.

Mama Yangu. I cannot remember when I forgot her and stopped asking for her guidance. I cannot remember when she stopped being my angel. I cannot even remember her smell.

Josephine, whom I failed. Her beauty was the only thing she cherished, and I robbed her of it.

Samuel, my friend, whom I killed.

And my Dada, my Dada Zakiya, the most important person in my life. The guilt I have carried since the watch incident has haunted me every moment, guilt that she does not trust me and hates me. I want to free her from my thoughts. I want to release her from my life. I take a good look at myself in the cracked mirror, and this time I look pale on both sides.

To forget all the sorrow that surrounds me, I spend more time in the evenings with Emanuel. I do most of the reading and he listens. He is a slow learner, or maybe I am a lousy teacher. I cannot compare myself with Dada Zakiya. She was natural, and everything she did came from a pure heart, purity I will never achieve.

Emanuel and I read *Alice in Wonderland* together, the book I cherish so dearly. It still carries Dada Zakiya's scent.

Later, when I am alone, I turn to the first page and read her message over and over:

For my best friend, Juma.

May you never stop here.

Love, hugs and kisses, Zakiya.

I cry and apologize to Dada Zakiya. "I am sorry!" Suddenly, I realize what she means to tell me.

Early the next morning, I go to the beach and notice that the tide is already high and the wind is up. The fishermen unlock the shed provided by the government to store their dhows overnight. They struggle with their dhows in the rough current. God seems angry today. I cling to my bag, making sure it is safe. In it is my most valuable possession, and the rusty coffee tin rattles. "I will be back in the evening when no one is around," I tell the ocean before heading to work.

A gust of wind sways the kiosk door. There is a loud thunderstorm. People gather on the side path, laughing and feeling lucky for the rains; the monsoon season has finally arrived. The day seems longer than it should be, probably because I am anxious. The weather has kept the tourists away and the Freedom Kiosk is not busy—Maria has only three appointments. I help Mrs. Scott sort the beads she has purchased from *duka ya shanga* by colour and size. In the afternoon, she shares her biscuits with Maria and me as we enjoy a cup of coffee. All day I attempt to let Maria know that I have the watch and what I intend to do with it, but I worry that she might change my mind or have her own ideas, so I let it be. Maybe I will tell her tomorrow after freeing myself from Dada Zakiya. My decision is final and I must do this.

The scent of earthy sand from the rain brings me immense peace. I walk to the beach, to the same spot where I let Mama's ashes free, the same spot where Dada Zakiya and I held hands and prayed for Mama and Dada Zakiya's father.

The dhows have been locked up and there are no fishermen to be seen. On the other side, the luxury water taxis line up. Many city people pull up in their cars, simply to take the water taxi to the resort for an evening of joyful dining and dancing. Rain or shine, nothing ever stops *Wahindi* from having fun.

The rain is heavy and the ocean feels alive. I stand by the shore, drenched, listening to the dancing waves create the sound of freedom. God is happy and blessing us. I smile and laugh, louder and louder. I pull the mirror out of my pocket and wash it in the ocean. I look at my reflection, and this time I am clean and bright on both sides. The monsoon rains have cleansed me, a heavenly moment that takes me to a serene and peaceful place. Now I am ready.

I remove the tin from my bag and pull out the watch, hang the watch belt over my fingers and close my fist. For a long time, I admire the dial shining over my knuckles. "I will make it tick for another fifty years," Dada Zakiya would say to me. Yes, Dada, yes, now I am going to make it tick forever. I think of Dada Zakiya, and I feel happy. Finally, I believe she has always trusted me.

I kiss the watch goodbye and get ready to throw it far to the other side of the ocean where Dada Zakiya is waiting to catch it. Louder thunder strikes, followed by another downpour, and the waves move the ocean closer to my feet. Seaweed covers my ankles. I fear that if I throw the watch close to the shore, it may wash back to the land. I walk farther into the ocean, up to my waist. As I swing my arm, a wave comes over me, washing my entire body under the sea. I swim up and stand ready to throw the watch farther into the sea, but this time the water has reached my chest and the ocean is much busier. A huge wave approaches me. I look up, look high, at a wave the size of a steamship. I am down, down deep, in the ocean. My fist opens up and Dada Zakiya's watch releases off my palm, as if she has reached me and touched my hand and accepted her gift back. I see her smile and thank me for finding it. Finally, I am at peace.

I struggle to swim up from the deep where the currents are strong. Every few strokes I take towards the shore, a wave takes me back deeper into ocean. I cannot see the shore anymore. I cannot see the water taxis. I am far, far away, distant from home. I gasp for air, I scream for help. My arms are tired and my legs tremble. I try to float but the waves pull me back into the depths.

This time, as I float, I see a shadow high above me, through the rain clouds, a glorious *kipanga*, falcon, flying towards the shore. I feel a burst of energy and my spirit lifts. I swim with huge strokes, strong strokes—nothing can stop me now—until I reach the shore. I lie face down on the sandy beach, exhausted. Above me I hear a sound, *kiki-kik, kiki-kik.* It is my *kipanga*, calling me from the top of a tall coconut tree. I feel her spirit, her strong *kipanga* spirit taking courageous flight. I spread my arms, stretching them wide, and burst into sound—*aaa, aaa, aaa*—loud, husky, clear.

I follow my *kipanga*, flying free.

epilogue
february 1992

ZAKIYA STANDS OUTSIDE the travel agency that was once Mama Fatima's hair salon. She touches the walls and closes her eyes. Yes, this was the salon. She can smell the peroxide, hear the laughter and giggles of the women.

But the street has changed. Ten years is a long time, she thinks to herself. Everyone has moved on, left the street, with the exception of the butcher, who does not remember her. "I am sorry, I can't help you," the butcher says. "Maria was a private woman, you know, so I don't know where she lives. Of course Juma, who didn't know Juma on the street? His life changed drastically when Mrs. Scott gave him the job. He worked for her for almost five years, I'd say." He looks up, trying to remember if it was indeed five years. "Then a few years ago, Juma mysteriously disappeared. One monsoon day, he left work but never reached home, and no one could locate him."

Zakiya blinks several times to prevent tears.

She walks the street for a good fifteen minutes, recalling her past, absorbing every scent. She apologizes to the street for leaving without saying goodbye. She sits on the footpath, her heart in pain. She pictures Juma next to her and tries to grab him so he does not leave her. She walks to the back of the travel agency and leans against a parked car. I can smell you, Juma, I can feel you. Where are you?

Back at her hotel, she hires a Jeep and driver to take her to Hamisi's village. A group of village women approach the Jeep when they see the foreign visitor. Zakiya tries to communicate in forgotten Kiswahili. "Hamisi, *una jua* Hamisi? Does anyone know Hamisi?" The driver joins in and helps with the translation.

The women look at each other in silence. Then one of them says, "Who are you? I can take you to his family."

Outside Hamisi's house, a little girl is playing with a broom. "Get your grandmother. Tell her she has a visitor," the woman says, and she leaves Zakiya by the entrance.

"Bibi, Bibi." The girl runs into the house, calling her grandmother.

Maria steps out of the house. She stands in front of Zakiya, stunned, and gasps. "Aai!" she screams. "Zakiya, is that you?" Zakiya, with her mouth open, nods. "I felt something good was coming my way today."

Zakiya rolls her eyes and places her hands on her head as though she is about to faint. Maria takes hold of her and they give each other a never-ending hug. "I searched for you and Juma in the city," Zakiya says. "My heart ached when I saw all the changes on the street. My gosh, Maria, you are a pleasant surprise. God loves me."

"This village is magical. There is always a pleasant surprise when you come here," Maria says and welcomes her into the house.

"Where is Hamisi?" Zakiya looks around with a smile.

Maria holds Zakiya's hand and softly pulls her down to sit, stroking Zakiya's arm a few times while she finds her courage. "Hamisi died two years ago, my child. After Mrs. Scott sold her kiosk, I retired and came here with my granddaughter to visit Hamisi. When I got here, I found he was sick. I stayed to tend him on his last days." She wipes Zakiya's tears. "Now I live here."

"That doesn't sound like a magical village to me." Zakiya is angry and her tears flow uncontrollably. "What pleasant surprise did you find? A sick man? I am too late, I am too late."

Maria lets Zakiya release her pain while trying to control her own. The girl jumps onto her bibi's lap to comfort her. Zakiya looks up and gives the girl a smile. "Come here," Zakiya says and lifts the girl in her arms. "You are as beautiful as your grandmother."

"Actually, she is very beautiful like her mother," Maria says.

"That's for me to judge when I see her," and she tickles the girl's arm. "Where is she?"

Maria's eyes fill with tears again and she stands up. "All we have is her mother's letter," she sighs. "Come with me."

Maria walks through the village at a fast pace. Zakiya runs after her, holding the girl's hand, wanting to ask Maria about Juma but feeling pain she does not understand. She is afraid to know and afraid to ask.

Maria stops at a school. A sign by the entrance, painted on a wooden board, reads *Shule ya Ndoto*, School of Dreams. Maria motions to Zakiya to follow her. The hallway of the school is cool, lit by filtered sunlight through the straw roof. Children are seated on benches having their storytime with the *mwalimu*, teacher, who reads with his head down.

"Baba, Baba," Maria's granddaughter says.

"What are you doing here?" The *mwalimu* looks up at the little girl.

Zakiya gasps. "Juma," she cries softly and looks at Maria.

Maria nods and smiles. "I told you, there is always a pleasant surprise in this magical village."

Juma drops *Alice in Wonderland* on the ground and freezes. Zakiya runs to him. The confused pupils stand up and gather around, wondering what is going on with their *mwalimu*. Zakiya strokes Juma's face, and Juma grabs her hand softly and holds her. Zakiya opens her sling bag, removes her stethoscope and puts it around Juma's neck. Juma touches the stethoscope and finally cries, "Dada Zakiya."

"I have always trusted you," Zakiya says and weeps in joy.

"I know, I know." Juma has difficulty speaking, but it does not matter. They both know and they do not need to say any more. They look into each other's eyes. Their spirits connect and their silence speaks.

the letter
july 1988

Dear Juma,

I am too ashamed to visit you at the kiosk and too ashamed to let anyone see me in this state. I am sorry, Juma. I was unfair to you and I was unfair to my own life. After we parted, I discovered that I was two months pregnant with your child, but I had already lost you. I took refuge at the Pombe House of Pleasures. Our daughter was born on 22.6.86. I wish I had realized earlier that love never dies and come back to you. But it is too late now. Life has been robbed from me and I am dying of AIDS. I am leaving our daughter at Maria's doorstep for her to bring to you. I am grateful to God for giving me two wonderful years with our daughter. Please don't be angry with me. Remember the night in the bus when you told me you loved me? I heard you. I was not sleeping, and I wanted to tell you that you are the only man I have ever loved. Forgive me.

Your love, Josephine

acknowledgments

First and foremost, I would like to thank my husband, Sadiq. You've been my best friend and my mentor ever since we met. This book would not have passed the first chapter without your guidance and encouragement. I am grateful to you for reading each draft of this book thoroughly as though it was the first time, and giving me true and honest feedback. You are my hero.

To my son, Zia, my other hero: thank you for listening to me babbling about my book late at night when only you would be awake and sharing your chocolate bars with me, and for reading the book, discussing the chapters and giving me feedback.

Thank you so much, Zia, for an excellent book cover design. Thank you to Zera Somjee, Zahra Jiwa-Karmali and Liz Martins for reading an early draft. Many thanks to the Port Moody Writers Group for their feedback and support. Thank you to my best friend, Laila Sekandari, for her wisdom. Thank you to my parents for their prayers. And thank you to all my well-wishers I've met along the way.

Lastly, thank you to my brilliant editor, Joyce Gram. You are truly magical. Your edits made my voice shine through without changing my writing style. You've been more than an editor in this process, and I can proudly call you my friend.

language glossary

ahsante sana	thank you very much
askari	security guard
baba	father
bahati	luck
banda	shed
barakat	prosperity
bendera	flag
beta	son, daughter
bhajia	Indian dumplings
bhangi	marijuana
biryani	Indian rice dish
bismillah	in the name of Allah
bwana	gentleman
chai	tea
chana bateta	chick peas and potatoes
chapa	slap
chh! chh! chh!	action: clicking tongue in regret
chhas	buttermilk
chor	thief
dada	sister
dadabapa	grandfather
dadima	grandmother
dagaa	sardines
daktari	doctor
dandhiya	dancing sticks/stick dance
duka	shop
elchi	cardamom

Ema!	Oh my!
fulana	under vest
futuru	breaking of fast
gandho	crazy, mad
Habari	What's up
haki ya Mungu	promise upon God's name
hapo	here
haraka	hurry
haya	okay
jambo	hello
jeera	cumin
kabisa	completely
kahawa	coffee
kakufa	dead
kanga	African shawl
karibu	welcome
kashiba	stomach is full
kemcho	how are you?
kesar	saffron
kikapu	basket
kipanga	falcon
kitenge	African kimono fabric
kitumbua	rice cake
kwaheri	goodbye
lakini	but
luving	cloves
madafu	coconut
magendo	bribe
maharagwe	kidney beans

malaya	whore or hooker
mama	mother
mandazi	doughnut
masala	spice
maskini	beggar
matatu	street bus
mbaya	bad
umerudi	returned
mchh!	sound of irritation
mehndhi	henna
mishkaki	barbeque beef
mitthai	Indian sweets
mittho	sweet
mogo	cassava
Muhindi	Indian
Mungu	God
Muzungu	European
mwalimu	teacher
mwizi	thief
mzee	old man
naomba	may i?
ndoto	dream
nini	what
ondoka	get out
paan	betel leaves
panwallah	person who prepares pan
pole	sorry
pombe	beer
potea	lost

putlo	omelette
rafiki	friend
safari	trip
safari njema	safe trip
samaki	fish
samhani	sorry
sema	say
shamba	farm
shanga	bead, bead necklaces
shikamo	greetings
shuka	African fabric
shukrana	thankful
shule	school
sokoni	market
susu	pee
tayari	ready
tulsi	basil
tumbo	stomach
ugali	corn meal
uhuru	freedom
uji	buttermilk
vikapu	baskets
vitumbua	rice cakes
Wahindi	Indians
wapi	where
Wazungu	Europeans
Ya khuda	Oh god
yangu	my

about the author

Farida Somjee was born in Mbeya, Tanzania. She grew up in the coastal city of Dar es Salaam. Many of her childhood memories resonate with her and come across in her writing. She moved to Canada in her late teens with twenty dollars in her pocket, a lot of dreams and God on her side. She lives in Vancouver, British Columbia, with her husband and son. *The Beggar's Dance* is her first novel.